JUST ONE BITE

An Edge of Night novel

Nicholas Scott

Dedication

I remember growing up and not enjoying reading. There were a few exceptions, Tolkien's *Lord of the Rings* and *The Hobbit*, James Fenimore Cooper's Leatherstocking Tales, but aside from that, my reading history would entail Little Golden Books and not much else. Then I saw the movie, *Stand By Me*. Something about it captured my imagination. I think it was an affinity for those characters. Suffice it to say I was compelled to venture to the bookstore, and Irene, the store clerk helped me find the very first book I'd ever bought on my own volition; *Different Seasons* by Stephen King. To say I was enamored, would be an understatement. My love of reading and writing is rooted firmly in the wondrous imaginings and literary creations of Mr. King. I'm certainly *not* his number one fan, but my gratitude knows no bound, because indeed he made in me a constant reader.

Copyright © 2015 Nicholas Scott

Just One Bite by Nicholas Scott

© 2015 by Nicholas Scott. All rights reserved.

Books By Nicholas Scott

Book One of the Fairweather High novels
Bright Lights Black Rainbows

Book One of Love & Kisses trilogy
A Kiss Is Just a Kiss
Kiss & Tell (coming in 2015)

Book One of Edge of Night trilogy
Just One Bite

JUST ONE BITE

An Edge of Night novel

Nicholas Scott

26 Letter Productions

Vampire - a preternatural being, commonly believed to be a reanimated corpse that is said to suck the blood of sleeping persons at night. – dictionary.com

CHAPTER ONE

Marked

Trystan

"Owww! Mother fucker! That fucking hurts, you asshole." I rubbed my arm where Jace had just bitten me. "What the fuck is it with you and biting. I swear to god, you've got some freaky ass fetish or something. You left teeth marks!" I twisted my arm so I could see the bite better. I was probably going to have bruise. "Fucker. One of these days your going to draw blood. And then I'm just gonna have to kick your ass."

Jace laughed. He always laughed at my threats. "Tough guy. The day you kick my ass, is the day I suck your dick." Jace shook his head, sending cold drops of water all over me.

It was my turn to laugh. "I think that's why you bite me. Cuz I won't let you suck me." I gave Jace a strong shove sending him backwards onto my bed and raced off to the bathroom. "You better be ready by the time I'm done with my shower!"

"Ready for what? To suck it?" He yelled from my room

"No idiot! For school, ya perv. You need a girlfriend, you're starting to sound a little desperate."

I closed the door to the bathroom, the warmth from his shower not quite dissipated. I rubbed a clear swath across the steamy mirror and glared balefully at myself. *You need a girlfriend?* Smooth. I gave myself the finger and turned on the shower, stripping out of my pajama bottoms. *You need a girlfriend? What the hell is wrong with you?* It was the last thing I wanted. Every time he had a girlfriend, I was in complete misery. It was hell on earth for me. *But hey, go ahead and make that suggestion.* I hung my head under the hot spray of the shower.

"Seriously? Again? I am so hating this song?" Jace reached for the stereo but I grabbed his hand away from the volume control.

"Nooooo. I love this song!" I raised my voice and sang along.

"You're so gay." Jace laughed as he got the better of me and turned downed the volume. "That song is gay."

"Oh? You're like the last person I'd come to for music advise." I looked at him with feigned disgust. "You know nothing, Jon Snow."

His laughter rippled through the car. "Just cuz you quote Game of Thrones doesn't change my mind." He reached back and snatched his backpack off the backseat then grabbed the door handle. "I'll see you in history." And then he was gone, dashing through the parking lot and up the steps throwing a few waves to friends as he disappeared. I sighed and grabbed my own backpack from beneath my feet. *Fuck*!

I didn't see her standing there, but when I opened the door, there she stood, seeming ethereal, almost translucent, the early morning sunlight glancing off of her. Her long dark hair shifted in the breeze, her eyes, the darkest brown I'd ever seen, appeared to look right into me. I couldn't help but think there was something familiar about her, but I couldn't quite put my finger on it. I looked up at the big red brick building as the bell rang.

"Excuse me." I tried to walk around her, but she reached a hand out and grabbed my wrist. The urge to pull away slipped from me as I stood in front of her, lost in her gaze. You would have thought when she leaned in to kiss me I would have pulled away. But I couldn't. I tried, or at least I wanted to pull away, but still her lips pressed against mine and then I had no control over anything. I kissed her back. It was amazing. Like the best kiss I could possibly ever imagine. And imagine I did, but it wasn't her I was kissing but Jace. I felt his lips, smelled his scent, strong and overwhelming, felt his hand at the back of my neck pulling me tight against him, felt him pressed against me, felt his excitement at the kiss. The moment was overpowering and when she pulled away, and she had to because I didn't want to let go of her, didn't even know that I was holding on to her, one arm pressed against the small of her back, the other at the back of her head, fingers twined through her hair. It left me breathless. She quirked a puzzled smile at me as she pulled away and broke contact. I didn't even realize I had dropped my backpack, but I bent to pick it up, when I stood she was gone. I could still smell Jace, his cologne filling my senses. I looked around dumbfounded, curious as to what had just happened. I heard the bell ring and it became apparent that I was the only one in the parking lot; just me, standing alone and a security guard who stared menacingly in my direction.

"You need to get inside." His stance was authoritative.

"Did you...?" I glanced around again, certain she had to be here somewhere. "D'you see a girl just now?"

He smirked. Like it was one of the most natural questions in the world. "Sorry Romeo. She's probably inside, just like everybody else. Everyone, except you."

I looked down; trying to look embarrassed and then headed towards the steps to the school. I glanced back curiously and saw him looking around, as if maybe he *did* see someone else. I reached up and rubbed at my neck. When I pulled my fingers away, they were slick and sticky. I gaped down at the sight of blood. Reaching up again I felt a sudden sting. I hissed and pulled my fingers away only to reach back again with tentative fingers. *Oh my god, she bit me.* Inside the main corridor, I rushed to the closest bathroom and examined my neck in the mirror. There was a smear of blood on my neck, but that was all. I wiped at it with a wet paper towel. Under the smear of blood, my neck appeared unblemished, perfectly normal. *What the fuck?* This was just weird. I wet a paper towel and cleaned my neck.

Biology class always put me to sleep. Okay, class in general, puts me to sleep. There was a problem with that. I have a tendency to dream of Jace all the time; almost every night if I were to be honest. It's sorta baffling because we spend most of our time together, so I can't imagine why my imagination needed any more time with him, but apparently left to its own devices, it's Jace Blackwell 24/7, on every channel. They weren't all, *those* kind of dreams. Mostly they were innocent, everyday dreams, with the occasional quirky thing, like being able to fly. One time, I dreamt we had both been killed. He had tried to save me from a killer and the killer had ripped his throat out and then proceeded to do the same thing to me, before I could help Jace. I remember waking with a jerk and calling Jace on the phone, at like 3:00 in the morning, out of breath and frightened. He answered groggily and proceeded to rip me a new one for waking him up.

Then of course, there were *those* dreams. I don't remember when I first had one and more than once I woke frightened and terrified as well.   Certainly confused uncertain as to why, because there was nothing terrifying about Jace. And nothing confusing about my feelings for him, but adding a sexual element baffled me. He was a big teddy bear really, in that oh-my-god-you're-sexy-as-hell sort of way. Course I had to keep those thoughts to myself. I don't know how he would react, just that I didn't think it would be good.

I didn't mind the dreams in which I knew I was dreaming. Like the one where we could fly, my subconscious seemed to tell me. Hey buddy, you're dreaming again. The one where we were killed, that one frightened me and stuck with me. It was so real, so vivid. And those dreams, well I didn't mind them at all. But waking up in the middle of biology with an erection and the image of Jace naked and just beyond my grasp certainly wasn't ideal.

"Mr. Cole?"

I looked up at Mr. Garrow. He had an expectant look on his face. Apparently he had asked me a question and wanted an answer. "Uhhhh. Two?"

A titter of laughter rippled through the classroom as I rubbed my eyes and discreetly readjusted myself.

"Mr. Cole. I realize I'm boring you. But perhaps you can hide it a little better, like the rest of your classmates."

"I'm sorry Mr. Garrow. I'll try harder to hide it." I grinned and grabbed my pencil and pretended to copy his scribble off the chalkboard.

"Can anyone give me an example of what a genetic trait is. And no," Mr. Garrow looked at me for emphasis, " two is not a trait." Another round of laughter filled the classroom. I tried to look abashed and pretended to scribble more. "This is simple biology. You should have learned this in junior high."

Several of my classmates raised their hands: mostly, the ones in the front row. Mr. Garrow pointed to Cassie Williams. She was a brain, probably the smartest person in class.

"We are diploid organisms, meaning that we received one set of genes, called alleles, from our father and the other set of alleles from our mother. The combination of these pairs of genes that we've inherited is called our "genotype. The genotype determines the actual traits (called the "phenotype") that we have; such as eye color, nearsightedness, and whether or not we have dimples" Cassie smiled real big and pointed to her dimples. "My dad has them, but my mother doesn't But dimples are a dominant genetic trait so since the phenotype is present, I automatically got them."

Half the class was staring at her like she had just spoken Russian or grown a second head. (I wondered if that was a dominant genetic trait.) But the majority had their phones, hidden discreetly under their desks, texting; oblivious of Cassie's answer, oblivious of everything around them but the 4 to 5 inches between their legs. There might have been one or two scribbling notes.

"Thank you Cassie. That is a wonderful example." Mr. Garrow turned and wrote the words: allele, genotype, phenotype, dominant trait and recessive trait on the chalkboard. A few more pens and pencils scribbled quickly. A few actually took quick photos with their phones of the chalkboard.

The bell rang and everyone grabbed backpacks and crammed phones into pockets.

"Tomorrow I want examples of what external factors may affect your genes." Mr. Garrow grabbed his eraser and went to work erasing everything he'd written during class.

Shoving my notebook in my backpack, I looked up and saw her, the girl from the parking lot. She was staring at me from the hallway. As soon as I noticed her she disappeared into the crowded hallway. I ran from my desk and stood in the doorway, blocking anyone from coming in as I searched for her. I didn't see her, but strangely enough, I could smell Jace. I scratched my head in confusion, glancing up and down the hall. I went back to my desk and grabbed my backpack and noticed a drop of blood on my desk. I reached out tentatively to touch it.

"Mr. Cole?"

I whipped around. Mr. Garrow stood behind me, his brow quirked questioningly. "Don't you have to get to your next class?"

I looked back, but didn't see any blood. "Uhhhh." I nodded in confusion. ".... I mean yes." I slung my backpack over my shoulder and rushed out of the room, looking back over my shoulder. Mr. Garrow stood at my desk, looking down, running a finger across my desktop. The weird thing was watching him bring that finger to his lips. I absently reached up to my neck but felt nothing.

History class was next and I plopped down next to Jace. "I'm having a weird day."

I looked over but Jace had his phone out, texting. I could tell he had just come from athletics. His hair was still damp from a shower and I could smell the Axe shampoo that he liked. I could smell his deodorant. I could smell him.

"Huh?" Jace looked up, appearing disoriented then realized I was there. "Trys?" He was looking at me like he didn't recognize me.

"I said, I'm having a weird day. This chick, this morning, out in the parking lot, she came up and kissed me. Like out of the blue. Never seen her before, in my life, and the next thing I know, she's got her tongue down my throat. And I think she bit me." I angled my head revealing my neck to him. "And then I saw her again in the hallway right after biology." I leaned in and whisper conspiratorially. "And..." I looked to my left and then right. "I think Mr. Garrow is a vampire." I was only half joking, but Jace looked at me like I was preaching the gospel from the pulpit.

Jace traced a finger along my neck, in the exact spot where I thought she had bit me. The sensation sent shivers racing through me. He shook his head and shrugged. "I don't see anything." He pulled his hand back slowly.

"Yeah, well. There was blood there this morning." I rubbed at the bite, absently. It tickled like an itch I couldn't scratch or maybe I was still feeling Jace's touch.

"Are you sure you didn't like *dream* it?" Jace looked at me. He knew I had a tendency to fall asleep during class.

"I didn't dream it! It was like right after you left the car this morning. I got out of the car like right after you and...and there she was. I tried to go around her and she grabbed my wrist and the next thing I know, it was like Wrestlemania in my mouth. One! Two! Three! And then she was gone. Like the wind. Kinda freaked me out. Then at the end of biology she was in the hallway outside the classroom staring at me. I tried to catch her, but she was gone again." I shook my head. "I'm not crazy."

Jace was looking at me like I was crazy. "Okay. Okay. You're not crazy. But let's just look at this logically."

You have to understand. When Jace says, we have to look at things logically; you know there's something wrong.

"First, when's the last time someone came up and kissed you. And you're mom doesn't count." Jace grinned. And if it weren't for that goofy-assed grin, I probably would have slugged him.

"Ha ha. You're a riot." I glared at him.

"Second. We were up awfully late last night. You know, with me kicking your ass so bad at World of Warcraft." He paused for affect. "What's more likely? Some girl, a complete stranger, I might add, comes up to you, and even more importantly, not me, and kisses you."

I started to respond but he didn't allow me.

"Or....Or..." He raised a finger to shush me. ."...Maybe, when you were in Economics this morning, the desk ever so inviting, ever so sleep inducing, you know, along with the drone of Ms. Apple, Maybe ,just maybe you might have fallen asleep and dreamed a little dream?" Jace liked being melodramatic at my expense, throwing in a few hand gestures as he nodded his head at his own explanation of events.

I could only glare. It made sense. I guess. I could have dreamed it. I did have that tendency. I reached up and felt my neck and felt nothing. Nothing that proved this strange girl had bitten me. Nor existed for that matter. And a dream would certainly explain why the only things I could smell was Jace. I felt a blush rise to my cheeks and said a little prayer of gratitude as the bell rang. I sank low in my seat, casting glances over at Jace as he pulled his history book from his backpack. He glanced over at me once, his blue eyes sparkling mischievously.

Jace

I think Mr. Garrow is a vampire.

Okay. Let's just get one thing straight, once and for all. Vampires are people too. No. No. Laugh about it all you want, but it's true. Sure, you've seen the movies, read the books, worn the wax teeth at Halloween, It's all such wonderful make-believe; until you wake up one day and it's happening to you.

And it isn't exactly the way you think. Oh yeah sure, there is that damned bloodlust. Some times it's all I can do not to drag someone into a closet and eat. But vampires have come out of the dark ages and into the 21st century like everyone else. Science has made great strides in remedying the bloodlust. As the pundits say "there's a pill for that."

Okay, and I'll be the first to admit that there are the proverbial bad seeds out there. But that can be said for everyone. And history has shown that we've had our fair share of issues. The black plague; completely *not* our fault. Just a few vampires taking advantage of the situation... And okay, yes, the Jamestown colony, might....*might* be laid at our feet....but all of that ....ancient history.

I mean, I wasn't even born then. I'm newborn, so to speak. I wasn't turned by some romantic pale fanged creature of the night. Nope. Born and raised and then along with puberty and body odor and zits, I get a small case of vampirism. It's genetic, as lady gaga would sing. Baby, I was born this way. So before you start getting any ideas, I just wanted to set the record straight.

I glanced over at Trys. He absently rubbed at his neck. I had told him there was nothing there, but the truth; I could see the mark. Not teeth marks, she wasn't trying to bite him, technically, just turn him.

Yeah, so okay, I had lied to Trys. It's not the first time, and it won't be the last. We've known each other since we were three. And contrary to popular belief; best friends lie to each other all the time. Sure the truth comes out, eventually, then you fight, make up and everything is right as rain. That's what best friends do. White lies are a part of the deal. No, those jeans don't make you look fat. No, you can barely see that zit. No I don't see any vampire ...

What I didn't understand and what had certainly taken me by surprise was the sudden anger, the sudden covetous jealousy concerning Trys. I already marked Trys as mine. It wasn't intentional when I did it, but now, all these years later, Trystan Cole was mine. And here comes this bitch, out of the nowhere, who has the audacity to try and mark him, to turn him.   I couldn't help but wonder what that meant. Why Trys? Why now?

I snuck another peek at him. I couldn't help but wonder what he felt when she tried to mark him.

CHAPTER TWO

Marked II

Jace

The pills were small and looked like cartoon characters. To the normal eye, you'd think I was taking a children's vitamin. I guess that's why they make them that way; to fool the average person. I swallowed two, chasing them down with a glass of water.

The pills go down dry, even with the water. They were highly concentrated doses of mitochondria; as the my dad liked to call it 'the body's cellular power plants.' All I knew is that it suppressed my bloodlust. I had to take them every morning otherwise I get jittery and if I waited too long, I could smell the blood in others, almost taste it.

I watched through the window as Trystan parked and made his way up the sidewalk. I couldn't help but smile. His hair was a complete mess. Even from here I could see he had missed one of the buttons on his cardigan. One of his pant cuffs was tucked in his sock. I watched him stumble and look to make certain no one had noticed, even though he was the only one out there.

I headed down the stairs as I heard him knocking.

I opened the door. Trystan stood there like he was still asleep.

"Don't you have a mirror?"

"Huh? What?" Trystan ran a hand through his hair.

I reached for him and set the buttons right on his cardigan then bent to fix his pant leg. "There. Much better." I was tempted to run a hand through his hair too, but fought the urge. I took his hand and dragged him inside. "Come on. Want some toast?"

Trystan had a thing for toast. I think if all there were to eat was toast, Trys would be perfectly content.

I dropped four slices in the toaster, pulled the butter from the fridge and looked at him again. "You look tired."

He rubbed his eyes sleepily and nodded. He leaned against the island, yawning over the toaster, watching as the bread slowly browned. He stared, captivated. When the toast popped up, he jumped. Then he went to work buttering, holding the first piece of buttered toast in his mouth as he slathered a second.

"Who kept you awake?" I asked it lasciviously, with a smirk, though knowing Trys as I did, no one had kept him awake. He had never had a girlfriend as long as I'd know him nor had he ever confessed to liking anyone.

Trys nearly choked on his toast, which told me, there was someone or something. I felt a hitch in my throat.

"It wasn't anyone. I just couldn't sleep. I kept having this dream, over and over that kept waking me up." He didn't look at me as he explained, but I noticed a hint of crimson in his cheeks.

"A dream, huh?" I grinned and he blushed even deeper. "Was it the girl from the parking lot?" I tried to say it like I didn't think I really believed there was actually a girl, even though I was afraid there was.

"Yeah." That was all he said as he bit into his third slice of toast, well bit would be an understatement as he practically devoured the slice whole. I'd grown accustomed to his peculiar eating habits and rituals.

"Did you do the nasty?"

He glared, darkly. "Shut up. And no, we didn't do the nasty." He did quotation marks with his fingers as he said nasty. "I mean, not really. She just kept kissing me. And..." He looked at me, oblivious of the toast crumbs and smudge of melted butter on his lips. "There was all this blood. I could smell it and taste it and it was all over everything." His eyes were hollow, his face pale and the piece of toast in his hand shook as he spoke.

I took a step closer to him and he leaned away from me. "Every time I closed my eyes, it's all I saw.

"Maybe you should stay home. You don't look so good."

I knew it was the girl, whoever she was. My mark protected him, but I didn't know what the effects would be, if she did bite him. It wasn't *if* it would change him, but rather *how*. I looked at him. Whatever effect, it wasn't in any obvious way, nothing I could see.

"Maybe she gave you mono."

"What?" He popped 4 more slices of bread in the toaster.

"You know...the kissing disease." I explained. My stomach was all jittery. I couldn't help but think this was my fault. I guess in a way it was. I mean, sure, if she had bit him; without my mark on him, he'd be way worse off. But now, I didn't know what to expect. He was showing symptoms of something, not vampirism, but certainly a reaction to her attempt. And, she had drawn blood.

I cringed at the thought of talking to my father. He would have answers.   But I knew I had to, just to know what I was going to have to do.

Trystan

I was so hungry.   I stared at the toaster, waiting for the second set of four slices to pop up.   Normally two slices will do the trick, at least until I get to school and could get a snack from the vending machines.   But after 4 slices I was still famished.   I mean it feels like I haven't eaten in days.   Not that I know what that feels like, but it certainly doesn't feel like I've just eaten 4 slices of toast.   And they didn't taste like anything.   I couldn't taste the butter or the bread.   It was bland

The toaster finally popped up four more slices of golden brown toast and I slathered a slice with butter, lots of butter and took several quick bites while slathering a second slice.

Jace gave me a strange look. "Are ya hungry there buddy?"

"What?" I looked at him. He was especially cute today. Jeans and a t-shirt never looked so good. I was certain he woke up looking like that. If he weren't so damned cute, I'd be disgusted by the whole notion. Whenever I spent the night, it was all I could the next morning to keep from jumping him. He was perfect. I felt stupid thinking that he was lovely. It sounded so.... feminine, but he was. His eyes were captivating. Mesmerizing. It was hard to look away. Not that the rest of him wasn't captivating as well. He had a certain scent that was uniquely him that drove me crazy. I could smell him now. The scent triggered an image from my dream.

The girl was there. Floating and beckoning me with outreached hands. Everything was dark except for her: she was surrounded by a halo of light, but the darkness around her was foreboding in its blackness. I felt myself wanting to go to her, but part of me fought it, sensing a danger that I couldn't quite recognize. But I felt it, as if the light blinded me to her true nature. Still I walked towards her, or rather it felt like I was floating and being pulled towards her, like a tractor beam or something. The closer I got, the stronger I fought until I was within her grasp. She pulled me to her, I felt her lips on me, kissing me; my neck, my shoulders, my jaw line and then finally my lips. I tried to pull away, but I felt one of her hands gripping my shoulder. The fear I felt was overwhelming. When I looked back, it wasn't her hands that held me firm, but Jace's and it was like an out of body experience, watching him kissing me, his arms wrapped around me, holding me tight to him. And then I saw the blood. We were drenched in it; our hands slick with it and the scent of it, suddenly so overwhelming, it made me want to vomit. I pushed away from him, slipping in the blood and falling down, blood splashing up and covering my hands, as if it were ankle deep and the ground was soft with it. And Jace stood there, looking down at me.

"You are mine and I am yours." That was all he said before he sprang on me, his teeth bared and I could see the fangs before I tried fighting him off, felt them plunge into my throat, and the only sensation I can remember was the scent of him. And I screamed, jerking awake, panting and sweating, my ears filled with the pounding of my heart.

I devoured the last piece of toast, averting my eyes from Jace. I contemplated putting a couple of more slices in the toaster. I was still hungry, but Jace was eyeing me like I might be a little crazy.

"You ready?" He grabbed his backpack and slung it over his shoulder.

I followed him out to my car. He stood on the passenger side staring at me, waiting for me to unlock the door.

"Helloooo.   Are you sure you're alright?"   Jace looked worried.

I tried to smile but my heart wasn't in it.   Something was seriously wrong.   I unlocked the door and climbed in, my muscles sore. It felt like I had the flu or something.

CHAPTER THREE

Marked III

Jace

I noticed her...or rather felt her, before I saw her.

I know it sounds cliché, but if you think about it, vampires, be they turned or born this way, their bodies are different. I mean there are some clichés that are completely wrong. That whole coming back from the dead is just make-believe. Fairy tales. Once you're dead, you're dead. It's as simple as that. Being bitten by a vampire doesn't kill you, unless that's the vampire's intent. No, quite to the contrary, the body just goes through a metamorphosis, and while you may appear back from the dead, the truth of the matter is, it's like a butterfly coming from a cocoon. I know, it's a bad analogy, digging yourself out of a grave is nothing like coming out of a cocoon, but you get the idea.

A vampire is more attuned to its environment. All of our senses, both physical and mental, are so much stronger. I couldn't tell you what the difference is, because I was born this way, but I can tell you this, with one whiff, I could tell you your cologne, your hair products, laundry detergent, body soap, deodorant, tooth paste, whether or not you've taken your vitamins, what you had for breakfast, lunch and dinner and whether or not you need to go to the bathroom. I know, it sounds a bit overwhelming, but like I said, I was born this way, so I don't know anything different. That's how other vampires notice other vampires. Has nothing to do with telepathy, but rather the scent. We can cover it up, to a degree, but the scent is so familiar, so innate to our very being, we can't help but notice it. It's almost tactile, palpable, that scent, almost makes it seem extrasensory.

She stood at the far end of the hallway, her eyes intent on me. It had only been a day since she had tried to mark Trystan and even from here I could smell the hormonal interaction lingering on her. I wondered if she had turned him on. She was beautiful. I could tell from where I stood, that she was a born vampire not turned. The body of turned vampire is not as efficient as that of a born vampire. Turned vampires have a stink, for lack of a better word, due to that inefficiency. The older the vampire is when it is turned, the more obvious the aroma. In a way, they smell almost human. Oddly, her scent suggested she had been turned recently, probably within the last year.

I watched her as she walked towards me, something feral in her eyes. And in case you're wondering, no, the crowds in the hall, didn't open up to her, leaving her path clear, nor did she appear as if she were floating. Quite to the contrary, she was bumped twice, got a hip check from one of the meaner cheerleaders who probably expected the crowd to give way to her and then was momentarily diverted by Zachary Holt who was clearly enamored with her. I could see the frustration in her eyes as she listened to him go on and on, inviting her to his soccer game and to a party and if she wanted to go to the Frozen Toad for some ice cream. After a perfunctory yes, she disentangled herself and made her way to me.

"You marked him?" Her eyes held a bit of confusion, a bit of accusation.

"Yes."

"He doesn't know?"

"No. I'll have to tell him now, thanks to you." I glared

I marked him a long time ago. It was an accident really. As I mentioned, we've known each other since we were three. Have gone to school together since kindergarten and I certainly couldn't imagine my life without him. I didn't think I was in love with him, you know from the very beginning. I just knew that he was my best friend and I loved him as such.

We were climbing trees out in the woods, daring each other to go higher and higher. I think we were only in 6th grade. By then I knew it was more than just friendship that I felt, but I really didn't understand it, certainly couldn't put it into words.   All I knew was watching him, wearing a tank top and basketball shorts, his chest and arms toned, his crotch showing a hint of a bulge, I was mesmerized. I couldn't help it. I guess that's why I slipped. I had a firm grasp on the branch above me but my feet dangled below as I bellowed for Trystan to help me.   I tried swinging my feet back up to the branches and I almost did but then I saw Trystan plummeting from his own perch above mine past me and to the forest floor. I remember yelling as I saw him hit, his body bounced. That's when I let go and crashed through the branches, I could feel them scratching my face and bare arms and legs.   I landed on my feet and in that moment, it didn't register what I had just done. All I could think of was getting to Trystan. The scent of Trystan was a cloud all around me.   My every sense was attuned to him. I thought I could hear his heartbeat, his breathing; something that seemed impossible to my sixth grade mind.   One of his arms was underneath him, bent at a horrible angle.   The other had a bloody gash the length of his bicep. His nose was bleeding. His tank top was torn and it looked like a branch was protruding from his ribs.

Like any sixth grader I yelled for help, yelled my throat raw. But no one came.

It was the first time I felt the bloodlust.   In one way it's hard to describe, but in another, it's not at all. It's like being horny. To my sixth grade senses, just starting puberty, I really didn't have a full grasp of that overwhelming sensation.   Getting the occasional boner out of the blue while sitting in math didn't quite describe it.   The bloodlust was all encompassing, overpowering, and transformative.   Had it been anyone else, I probably would have killed him.   I admit it; I tasted him.   It scared the hell out of me.   I scrambled back and stared at him laying there, his quick shallow breaths the only sound I heard outside the blood pounding in my ears.

The woods were closest to my house. After the initial shock of his fall and then my tasting him, I knew I had to get him home. He wasn't that much bigger than me, but I was just a kid. I didn't know how I was going to carry him; I just knew I had to before he died. He was much lighter than I had expected. He wasn't completely unconscious as he wrapped his arms around my neck. He grimaced as I trudged over the terrain as fast as I could, his grip tightening and slackening in turn.

Once we reached the clearing I yelled as loud as I could. My voice was already hoarse and raw, but my yell seemed to echo and reverberate all around me. My father was at the back door and then racing towards us. Without even slowing his stride he picked us both up and raced back to the house.

"What did you do?" My father was looking at me, concern in his eyes. We were in his office, me sitting in the big Lazy Boy, him sitting on the corner of his desk.

"He fell from the tree and..."

"No. What did you do? I need to know Jace."

"I don't know." And I didn't really. "One second I was checking to see if he was alright, and then I was tasting his blood. The big gash on his arm, there was so much blood. I don't know why..."

"It's alright Jace." My father pulled me to him in a hug and I wrapped my arms around him, my eyes closed tight.

"Is he gonna be alright?" The words were muffled in his shirt.

He pulled me back so he could look at me. "Yes. He's going to be just fine. More than fine. I can't explain right now, but you have to promise me, you will not tell anyone, not even Trystan what happened out there. He fell and you carried him home. That's all. Nothing else. Promise me Jace."

"I don't understand."

I heard someone running. I looked at my father.

"Promise me."

I could only nod as Trystan came into the office, his cheeks flush, his eyes lit up. He jumped into my lap and planted mock kisses all over my face. "My hero!"

I pushed him out of my lap. "Get off me you 'tard." He landed on his ass but laughed anyway. I tried to laugh with him, but it sounded hollow.   He held out his hand for me to help him up. The gash on his arm was gone, all that remained, a small pink scratch. I stood up and pulled him with me. I hugged him awkwardly "I'm glad you're okay."

All of his other injuries were gone. No scratches, nothing broken. I looked at my dad, over Trys' shoulder as I felt Trys wrap his arms around me.

"Promise Me."

I nodded again

Tristan's mother drove over and picked him up.   She smothered me with hugs and thanked me so many times I lost count, all the while Trystan kept saying it wasn't so bad. "All I have is this one little scratch."

That one scratch wasn't the length of the gash in his arm, but rather the length of my lips, the length of my blood kiss.

That's what my father called it. After Trystan was gone, my father and mother had "the talk". Only this talk wasn't about puberty and sex and girls, but instead about vampires and bloodlust and about my blood kiss.   That I had marked him as mine.   Like puberty, sex and girls, I didn't really understand everything they were telling me. But the one thing I knew and understood completely was that Trystan Cole was mine.

CHAPTER FOUR

A Soul Deep Yearning

Porphyria is implicated in the origin of vampire myths because people with the disease tend to avoid the sun due to blistering and desire iron rich foods (blood and meat) due to their enzymatic deficiency. - Wikipedia

Jace

Trystan absently scratched at the small scar on his arm; my mark.   It looked like an ordinary scar, a pale blemish on his otherwise flawless skin; a blemish that he constantly attempted to cover up.   He'd even gone so far as to apply different ointments and creams that were supposed to remove scars and stretch marks, but to his frustration, nothing seemed to work. My fallback response that it could have been worse didn't seem to lessen his discomfort. I resorted to calling it his birthmark, which in essence was true.

I couldn't help but grin at his vanity, something he denied when I pointed it out to him, but I was certain, in his heart of hearts, he recognized it too. He had every reason to be, if one could have a reason to be vain.   My jealousy knew no bounds when it came to him. From his looks, which captivated and mesmerized me.   He could quiet a room walking into it...a subtle almost imperceptible quieting that rippled through a room not unlike the Doppler effect; growing more palpable the closer he came. He was oblivious of this effect he had on people, which made him all the more appealing.   As much as his appearance caused in me a great covetous jealousy, it was his unconscious charisma and charm, his siren's song, if you will, that drew the unsuspecting close to him. His voice, a sonorous enchantment that pulled your eyes just as his appearance did, seemed to befuddle and mystify. It wasn't those poor enamored souls that I was jealous of, but rather, the mirroring of affection that he intuitively emanated, which further cemented their regard for him, that affection that I craved solely to be mine.

I couldn't help but grimace at the notion that these traits were just those that were the alluded characteristics of a romantic vampire. The thought gave me pause. Did I do this to him with my blood kiss? Was the blemish, which he so despised the source of his almost otherworldly beauty and allure. Was his siren song, my doing?

"Hellooooooooo."

The fry hit me in the forehead, bringing me out of my reverie.

"Where the hell did you go?" Trystan was looking at me, armed with another fry. "You haven't heard a word I said."

"What?" I felt the blush in my cheeks.

"Exactly. Here I am pouring out my soul…"

"I'm sorry. It's been a long week."

There was no real anguish in his voice and his eyes twinkled mischievously. "A long week? A long week? You want a long week. I've had three tests since Wednesday, one of which I forgot all about, damn statistics, like we're ever going to use that again." He rubbed his eyes then sent a hand through his hair, pulling his bangs back. "Oh and a pop quiz in Spanish." He shook his head. He'd made a 42. "And let's not forget the mono scare from the crazy girl who bit me.… And she did bite me, and she was real, whether you believe me or not…" He absently rubbed at his neck.

"Okay. Okay. I told you I believed you!"

"You were just saying it to shut me up. I …"

I looked up and Trys was staring over my shoulder.

"What?" I turned to look behind me and caught her scent.

"No. Don't look. It's her." I turned back as he grabbed my arm and nodded his head in her direction. "The one with the black hair. Look. Look now."

I pretended to scan the cafeteria, but I knew where she was, her presence a lighthouse beacon in a sea of people. I wasn't the only one who noticed her. She drew stares, much like Trystan did. Zachary Holt was with her and from the scent of him; I knew she had turned him.   He looked ravenous, anguished that every person he passed was an edible distraction, but he seemed compelled to follow her. She let her hand linger behind her and he clutched at it, grabbing at it like a lifeline, bringing an inner peace that eased his struggle with the blood lust. But I could sense his agitation in a pungent plume of pheromones wafting about him. I was puzzled by her actions. Why would she bring him here so soon after his turning? It was only the sudden scent of blood that pressed me into action. Jumping from my seat, I reached across the table and grabbed Trystan by the arm, pulling him towards the closest exit. The blood was hers, the scent strong and growing stronger as she approached. But, I could smell his too, the death of the old cells as his white cells destroyed his healthy ones and I could smell the newly transforming vampire blood pulsing through his veins.

I felt my pulse quicken, pounding inside my head and a rush of adrenalin that triggered a sense of hysteria. I felt Trys jerk his arm from my grip. Looking back at him, I watched him rubbing the red mark where I had gripped him. "What the hell?"

"You need to get out of here. Right now."

Trys looked flabbergasted. "What? Why?"

"Just trust me.   I know it sounds crazy, but you're not safe right now.   You need to go. Run!" I gave him a little shove, though stronger than I intended, which sent him sprawling on the cafeteria floor.

"What the fu…"

I turned back towards the girl and Zach, taking a stand in their path. I looked back. "Run Trys." He scrambled to his feet and he looked like he was about to argue but then shook his head and disappeared through the double doors. The relief I felt was momentary then I refocused my attention on the approaching danger. The adrenalin surge had triggered my bloodlust and try as I might to fight it; still I felt my fangs pressing against the inside of my lips. My senses, which are acute during the calmest of situations, were now so strong I was suffering from sensory overload and a feral urge for blood coursed through me. With each heartbeat, like an incoming tide, the urge overwhelmed me. I felt powerless against the onslaught and the internal metamorphosis assailing me.

Made vampires are strong. They're given a preternatural strength from their maker that redefines, recreates on a molecular level, their very being. The metamorphosis is quick and it feels like a ravaging fire: a fever that wracks the body, debilitating it, burning away the humanity within. They say that the bloodlust of a made vampire runs deeper to make up for this lost humanity, like a phantom limb, the body feels that humanity or the loss of it, like a phantom limb, and craves it all the more and it's only way of retrieving any sense of that old humanity is the drinking of blood, the devouring of that life force, quenching a soul-deep thirst.

Fortunately born vampires are stronger.

To the untrained eye, what followed was just your average cafeteria brawl. Zach Holt jumped at me, with a savagery that might not have been witnessed by anyone but me, but the hunger in his eyes was all consuming and blatantly obvious to me. I wasn't his primary target but rather Trystan. And there was no way in hell he was going to get to Trystan with me alive. I was slammed against the wall with a brute force that knocked the air from my lungs. It was dizzying and I embraced fully my instinctual response to the attack and flung myself at him with abandon. The struggle to maintain control, to fight my inborn nature, was gone. If Mr. Garrow had not pulled us apart, and he was the only one who could, Zach Holt would have been dead.

"Enough." Mr. Garrow shook me, bringing me back to my senses. I gulped in air, my heart raced, pounding so strongly it hurt.

Zach seemed dumbfounded. He was bloodied and slouching against a cafeteria table, his eyes empty but searching. It was only then that I noticed; she was gone. Zachary was a distraction, proverbial cannon fodder and I had fallen for it. I could smell neither Trys nor the girl. I couldn't help but wonder why she was so intent on taking him, making him hers and all I could think of was getting free of Mr. Garrow's grip and finding them.   My mark protected him from most things, but not everything.

Mr. Garrow held me firmly by the collar of my shirt

"Jace? What's going on?"

I nodded towards Zach. "She turned him."

Mr. Garrow's eyebrows rose. "She? She who?"

"I don't know. She. She tried to turn Trystan, Monday."

"What do you mean, she tried?"

"In the parking lot on Monday, when no one was around, she tried to turn him. But... He's marked." I remembered my father's words from so long ago.

He looked at me then, eyebrows lifted, enlightened by my revelation.   "Marked?"

"Mr. Garrow, I really have to go. I'll try to explain later, but right now, she's after him and he has no idea what's going on."

I pulled free from his grasp and raced in the direction that Trys had gone.   His scent, as well as hers, was prevalent in the hall and the path the scent left was clearer. I followed it blindly. I could sense his confusion in the scent but I also picked up the scent of fear. What surprised me was that the fear was primarily hers, not his.

Trystan

"You don't know what he did to you, do you?"

I looked at her.   Her smile was sinister as she stalked closer.

"What are you talking about? Did to me?"

She weaved her way through the desks in the empty classroom. She stopped a few inches from me and pulled my arm up and turned it to reveal the scar.   She ran red painted fingernails across the scar; the sensation sent a chill rippling through me.   Her grip tightened as I tried to pull my arm back. "It looks plain enough. A simple scar." She looked at me then, her eyes piercing and intense in their depth. "Remember."

"It is a scar. I fell from a tree when I was 10.   Cut my arm." I remembered falling as easily as waking up this morning.   The tree was the tallest we had found and climbing it seemed the most natural thing to do.   We were 10 and Jace climbed fearlessly. There was no way I would let him get the better of me so I raced past him, higher into the tree. When I heard him yell for help, I lost my grip and fell.   Past him, past his outreached hand, down and down until I struck earth and everything went black.   But before everything went black, I remembered Jace jumping down after me; a slow motion special effect relegated to my dreams.   Which is what I thought it was, a dream, a 10 year-old imagination running wild.

"You don't know who he is. What he is."

"What?"

"Your friend." There was such disdain in her voice. "He's marked you. Made you his own. His little play thing. You will never love or want another. Only him. That is what the mark does." She smiled, heartlessly. "I see it in your eyes. You think you love him." Her laugh was cruel. "He stole your free will from you."

"Trys?" Jace stood in the doorway. "Move away from her."

I didn't realize we were so close.   She was pressed against me, her hands rested on my shoulders pulling me closer to her. I felt her breath on my neck.   "If you want your freedom, come to me."

I felt her jerked away from me. One moment she was there and in the next instant she was flung against the far wall with a crash.   "Stay away from him!"

She rose, unhurt, while the sheetrock behind her was caved in where her body had struck it and a bookshelf leaned haphazardly, books sliding then falling to the floor. I didn't know what was happening, didn't understand how she was not hurt or how Jace had been able to throw her with such force. Baffled, I watched her race from the room. I turned to Jace.

His proximity overwhelmed me. The heat emanating off of him, his scent enveloped me and I was compelled by a surge of arousal, a stir of unquenchable lust flowing through me, that I couldn't help but reach for him and kiss him. His arms quickly surrounded me and pulled me tight. I couldn't get enough. And in that moment, every desire, every want, every physical need I had, hungered to be fulfilled. It felt like a fire blazing inside of me, burning so hot that I forced Jace away from me.

"Holy shit! What the…what the hell was that?" I panted the words, doubled over, leaning against the wall, my hands supporting me at my knees. Even as I was bewildered, I struggled even more so with the need to do it again. I had always wanted him but never in my wildest of imagination had I ever all but forced myself on him. "I'm sorry Jace. I'm sorry Jace." The words were a whisper as I looked up at him. His head was ducked away from me. I could see his shoulders heaving as he breathed. "Jace? Jace, I'm sorry. I didn't mean…" The words froze in my throat. Jace looked up at me. His lips were red; too red, blood red.

CHAPTER FIVE

A Soul Deep Yearning II

Jace

Trystan scrambled back or at least tried to but his back was already against the wall.

"Trys... I...."

"You're bleeding."   He took a tentative step towards me.

I reached up absently and wiped at my lip. I looked at my hand, my fingertips bloody.

I could taste him and suddenly there were images, memories; flashing through my mind, making my heart race. The first ones were simple hazy memories; parks and play grounds, sand boxes and swings and slides and sharing graham crackers and juice, the sound the straw makes when the juice box is empty.   The first time he spent the night and we played video games and built a tent with my Teenage Mutant Ninja Turtle sheets, ate grilled cheese sandwiches my mother had made. And then we were ten and the images solidified until my imagination let me feel the branches in my hands as we climbed and feel the sunlight on my shoulders and hear the cracking snap of the branch and Trystan fell beyond my reach.   And the first and only other time I had tasted him. Shivers rippled through me and I staggered back, the sensation triggering a hunger.

"Trys, I need to tell you something. And it's going to sound crazy. Just promise me you'll listen. Until I'm done."

Trystan nodded, taking another step closer to me, his trepidation all but gone. A moment ago he was kissing me and then he was pressed against the wall pushing me away from him. I noticed his lips were red, noticed the stain of blood from when he kissed me.

"That girl..." I paused, nodding in the direction she had run. *You cannot tell anyone.* That inner voice sounded distinctly like my father's and I could feel the import of what he was saying even now. I sighed and looked back at Trystan. "She's a vampire. "

"Wait."   Trys absently rubbed his neck. Realization blossomed in his eyes and he puffed out his chest with validation. "So she did bite me! I knew it. I told you!"

His vindication was just a little bit annoying.

"Trys. Would you shut up a minute and listen. Didn't you hear me? She's a vampire. She tried to make you one."

. "I told you." He muttered again.

"I know! She bit you! I knew all along. Even when you couldn't see the bite, I could see it. I know! If it wasn't for me, you'd be out there somewhere probably biting somebody else." I had stepped up to Trystan and pinned him against the wall. I don't know why I was yelling, except I did. Being this close to him was always difficult.   The warmth from his body, his scent so potent and his taste still so fresh, I wanted nothing more than to kiss him.   God knows why, but I fought the urge, which infuriated me.

He started to lean into me but then stopped.   "Wait. You said she was a vampire?"

"Yes!"

"A vampire?"

"Yes."

"You're joking, right?"

I shook my head.

"How can she be a vampire? Vampires aren't real."

"How do you know they're not real; just because you haven't seen one? News flash, you saw one. And she bit you. She tried to turn you into a one."

His vindication had all but dissipated. In it's place was an angry skepticism. "Okay, let me get this straight. This chick, tries to seduce me and bites me in the parking lot, in broad daylight I might add, cause she wanted to turn me into a vampire."

"Yes."

I hated the look in his eyes, cynical and angry, daring me to keep going with this ridiculous farce. "Do you know how crazy that sounds? I know. I know I said that I thought Mr. Garrow was a vampire, but I wasn't serious. And now you're telling me vampires are real."

"Yes."

I could see his frustration growing with each yes. I guess I'd be frustrated too, if I were in his shoes.

"So how come I'm not a vampire? I mean. She bit me, right? Shouldn't I be like hiding in the crawl space under the house or hanging from the rafters of an old abandoned barn until sundown? I can't wait to turn into a bat."

I hated all that fictional nonsense. I couldn't help but blame Stephen King and his *Salem's Lot.* Trys and I had read it one summer, it was one of his favorite books "Well...normally, I guess you would be a vampire but you're protected."

"Protected? By who?"

I reached for him and took ahold of his arm and turned it to reveal his scar, just as she had. "By this." I ran a thumb across the scar.

Trys pulled his arm from my grasp. "By a scar?" He shook his head because he knew that that meant one thing. Me.

I shook my head at his expression and pushed forward with my explanation. "I didn't know what I was doing. You fell and you would have died.   My dad told me I couldn't tell anyone. Not even you. I wanted to tell you.   So many times we talked about it.   How you fell.   How all you got was that scar.   When the truth was so much different." Everything came out in a rush of words and Trys stared blankly, doubting my sincerity. "I didn't do it on purpose. You weren't moving and there was so much blood and I..."

"What? Turned me into a vampire?" His words echoed in the empty room, his anger palpable. "That means..." I saw the proverbial light bulb, the moment of realization. "*You're* a vampire?"

"No. I mean yes." I wanted to yell with my own frustration. "I didn't turn you into a vampire. Obviously. I…"

His eyes rounded. "For how long? Who turned you into a vampire?"

"I was born this way." I thought, for just a moment, there was a smirk and I knew, just knew he was suddenly listening to Lady Gaga in his head. But then he shook his head.

"I don't get it. Vampires are supposed to be…"

I shook my head. I really haven't had to try and explain it to anyone. "It's all make believe or… I don't know; it's hard to explain. I can take medicine for some stuff. Like I don't have to drink blood all the time to live. I take a pill that forces my body to make more red blood cells. I take another pill for porphyria, which counteracts my sensitivity to sunlight. Trys…I… "

"How come I'm not a vampire?" He looked at the scar on his arm. "Is this where you did it? Bit me?"

There was an accusatory tone to his voice, as if despite everything that had just happened, he didn't believe me "I didn't bite you. I mean…I don't really know what I did. But I didn't bite you. Not like a vampire bite."

Trys was examining the scar. A scar he'd had for over 7 years and he examined it like it was the first time he'd ever seen it.

"My dad called it a bloodkiss."

At the word kiss, Trys paled. He seemed to have forgotten that just a moment ago he had kissed me.

He tentatively placed fingers to his own lips, touching them, his finger tips coming away red. His eyes rounded again at the sight of it. He made a sudden gagging sound and doubled over with dry heaves.

CHAPTER SIX

A Soul Deep Yearning III

Trystan

I see it in your eyes.   You think you love him, that you've always loved him. He stole your free will from you.

I had always loved him, for as long as I could remember. And now, if I believed her, it was because of what he did to me. It wasn't real. He made me love him. I don't know why I was suddenly furious, but I was.   Our whole friendship was a lie, ever since the accident. Was I under a spell? I shook my head. That sounded stupid. I looked at Jace and felt it, the pull I felt whenever I was around him.   I didn't feel it around anyone else.

"What did you do to me?"

Jace looked dumbfounded at the anger in my voice. "I... I saved you." His voice was a whisper. He tried to look me in the eye but ducked his head and looked at his hands. "If I hadn't done it; marked you, you would have died." He shrugged his shoulders and then looked back up at me, his eyes glistening as he fought back tears. "I saved you."

I shook his head "You made me love you!" I wiped angrily at my lips. "I kissed you because of how you make me feel. What you made me think I felt. And it's all a lie!"

I shoved him with those words, then shoved him again and swung a fist. I missed him, as he stumbled back, his feet tangling with one of the desk chairs. Sprawled on the floor, he looked up at me in shock. The hurt in his eyes gave me pause.

"I made you love me? You love me?" Jace up righted the chair he had stumbled over and sat down. "You love me?" His eyes were incredulous.

I drew a hand across my face and looked down at him. Shit Shit Shit. I can't believe I just said that. "You know what I mean."

Jace shook his head. "I know what 'I love you' means, but I don't know what it means when you say it."

"Just forget I said anything."

"Oh yeah, like that's gonna happen."

"Well it doesn't matter. Since I don't have any control over it anyway." All I wanted to do was crawl under a desk somewhere and hoped Jace went away.

"Trys. I know that look. You can be pissed at me. Pretend I'm not here. But it doesn't change what you said. And it doesn't change what I feel."

"What you feel?" Jace stared up at me from his seat and smiled and I practically melted. The fucker.

"I've been in love with you for...I don't know how long. My whole life. When we were little, I just thought I wanted you to be my best friend and that you were the only person I would ever need. When I did what I did, I was saving my best friend. I didn't even know what I was then. I didn't know until afterwards, until my dad explained it to me." The hurt in his eyes was gone. "I won't deny, I want you to love me." His smile was back. "I want you to want me, I want you to be turned on by me. But if you think I have any control over how you feel, you're wrong. Just like you don't have any control over how I feel. It just is."

"It just is." I mocked. "Jerk."

"What?"

"You.   You.   You."   *Fucker.* I thought.   "You don't get to tell me something like that.   You've gone out with I don't know how many girls" It's 11, by the way.   "And you're going to tell me you've been in love with me your whole life? You're such an asstard."

I think Jace wanted to yell.   His frustration was so blatantly obvious he had to take a second to calm down, to take a deep breath and then he started to explain like he was speaking to a 5 year old.   "Look. My dad said I had to act normal. My whole life has been a secret since I was 10, even from you. I couldn't tell you any of it. My best friend." Jace smiled mischievously "Do you know how awesome it would have been for me to be able to tell you that I saved your life. Brought you back from the precipice of death."   Jace raised his arms dramatically then shook his head.   "But no, all I get is 'I fell from a tree, twenty feet, and all I got was this scar'. Like you were some superhero."

"Act normal? You just told me you're a vampire, for God's sake!" It felt stupid to throw that in his face, stupid and just a little bit surreal. My best friend was a vampire! Add to that, I had no idea, as close as we were, as much time as we spent together and I had no inkling.

"You know what I mean, Trys."   His shoulders dropped.

I still wanted to be pissed at him.   I wanted to shake him and yell at him and any number of other things to show him I was still pissed, that he wasn't the only one that was frustrated. But I wanted to kiss him again too.   Cuz that first one was like unfffffff.   Seriously.   It wasn't the cliché fireworks and romantic ballad in the background.   No…it was way past that. I looked around us, at the open door to the hallway. Walking over to it, I pulled it closed and turned around and found Jace right behind me.   "Oh. Hi." I swear to God I could feel my heart beating in my chest.

"Hi." Jace has this adorable smirk he gets, like he knows something. And I wonder if maybe he can read my mind.

"So yeah." I start hesitantly, scratching the back of my neck.   "I was thinking maybe we should try something.   You know, make sure it wasn't a fluke."

"Make sure what wasn't a fluke?"

"Forget it."

"No. No. Tell me." Jace stepped closer.

"What I felt." My ears were hot and I could feel the blush rise in my cheeks.

"Okay. Like what?" That smirk was even bigger. I wanted to hit him. Not as much as I wanted to kiss him, but still, you know that feeling.

"Like maybe I kiss you again. And see what it feels like."

"You want to kiss?" He sounded doubtful, despite the knowing smirk. Still, considering a minute ago he was telling me something seemingly implausible, I could understand his uncertainty. I was feeling it too.

"Uh huh." I nodded vigorously as he stepped even closer. I could feel the heat rolling off of him. I tentatively reached for his hand and took a hold of it only to let go and then grab it again. He grabbed my other hand and wrapped it around his waist. I needed no more prodding and pulled him against me. We both laughed a little, nervous laughter. I could tell, or rather could feel he was into it, at least as much as I was suddenly into him.

I admit I've liked him for as long as I can remember, but I can honestly say I've not felt this when around him. Sure, I've had dreams, but my waking hours aren't wrought with sexual desire. Not this. I put a hand on his chest and could feel his heart beating. He leaned into me, his crotch grinding subtly against me. I felt his hand slide into my back pocket as he pulled me even tighter against him. I think I might have squeaked a little bit before he finally kissed me. It was a tentative kiss, at least it started out that way, but with each passing second he grew bolder. His hands pulled at me, my hand on his chest gripped his shirt and pulled him closer and I forgot everything as we both lost ourselves. I was slammed back against the door, let loose another squeak and gasped for air as his mouth all but covered mine. He was grinding harder against me and a hand snaked down between us and I felt him grab me. I think he was bound and determined to get as many squeaks out of me as possible.

I had to shove him away from me. I was panting. "Okay…. Time…. Out…." Each word was followed by another gulp of air. "So… Yeah."

Jace's hands were reaching for me. Barely grasping, tugging at my shirt, at the waist of my jeans; his fingertips touching me all over. I had to keep my hands on his chest, forcing him at arms length.

"Holy hell! What are we doing?" I was breathless.

"Kissing." He said it like it was the most natural thing in the world.

I couldn't help but nod. It was my idea. I shook my head. "That wasn't kissing. That was…"

Jace started to lean into me again.

"No. Stop. Not here."

I couldn't help but laugh as he whined. "You're such a tease."

"I'm not a tease. The bell's about to ring and if we keep going I don't think we're going to hear it."

"Fine. Let's go home."

"I can't." I didn't dare let him persuade me.   One more kiss, even the start of one more kiss and there was no telling what I'd be willing to do. Jace leaned into me again. "You stay right there, mister!"

He whined again.   "Fine. I can't believe you're going to make me walk around the rest of the day with a case of blue balls."

I laughed again.   "Why don't you just go in the bathroom and knock one out."

Jace grabbed me by the shirt and pulled me against him. "Why don't you come with me and help." He said with a husky whisper. He thrust his crotch against mine and I had to close my eyes and breathe because I was so turned on I think I was about to make a mess. He was nipping at my lips, quick fast little kisses and I felt my resolve dwindling.

"Jace. You need to sto…"   His hand was at the base of my neck, fingers playing with my hair, his eyes intent on mine. He pulled me into another kiss and instead of fighting it, I push against the door and we banged our way through the classroom, knocking a couple of chairs and desks and the bookshelf next to the window until I had Jace pressed against the windows. Two can play at this game. He had a hand slipped into the back of my jeans and grabbing my ass, while one of mine had worked a couple of buttons open and had slid inside his shirt.   I kissed him hungrily, our tongues lapping at each other, tasting each other. I softly bit his lower lip and when he bit mine in return, I felt a sting and tasted blood. Then he pushed me away; hard enough I almost fell.   His breathing was so intense; I thought he was hyperventilating. I took a tentative step towards him but he shook his head and pointed towards the door, gesturing for me to leave. His eyes were blood shot and he was pale. He gripped the windowsill, stared straight down at his chest and took deep slow breaths. After several breaths he slumped down to his knees.

"Fuck."

"Are you okay? You're not gonna vamp out on me are you?"

Jace lifted his hand slowly and shot me the bird.

"You looked like you were about to eat me. How is it, you've date elev.... so many girls and have never eaten one?" I slumped down next to him and propped my head on his shoulder.

"Something happened.   Something that's never happened before." His bangs were sweaty and sticking to his forehead, but the color had returned to his cheeks.   He reached up and touched his lips. "You bit me."

"You bit me too." I ran my tongue across my lips but didn't feel anything.

"No. I didn't." He pulled his fingers away revealing a smear of blood. "That's the second time you've done that."

I remembered the taste of blood; the taste of Jace's blood. "This can't be good."

CHAPTER SEVEN

A Taste for Blood

Jace

Was he turning? I couldn't tell. He smelled the same. No 'vampire' smell going on, he smelled the same as always.

I couldn't help but smile. As far as I knew, he hasn't bit anyone. Just me. I felt foolish at the singular pride I felt in that. Or maybe it was the kissing, the oh-my-god-it-made-my-toes-curl kissing. I shook my head, trying to get the image, the sensation out of my head was impossible. I couldn't believe we had done it. I mean it was Trystan. Growing up together, he was like my brother, more than that, he was my conscience, my voice of reason, and I've known that I loved him, but I tried not to think of him that way. As much as I wanted to, as much as I craved him, I did the last thing I should have done.

My father was silent. He looked at me and he was not the least bit happy.

"Okay, just start from the beginning."

I told him about the girl, her initial interaction with Trystan, and later when she approached me and asked if I had marked him and then the attack in the cafeteria.

"You said she wasn't turned?"

I nodded.

"And she knows of the bloodkiss. Of Trystan being marked." He sort of said it to himself as he paced behind his desk.

"And you say she turned someone." My father was matter of fact in his questions.

I nodded. "Yes. Well I don't know if it was her, but…"

"How recently?"

"Well it had to be within the last couple of days. He was completely normal when he asked her to go to his soccer game."

"How was he acting this morning?"

"Like he was going through withdrawals. He was all shaky. And pale. But he was already strong."

"And her?"

"All I remember is her coming into the cafeteria and Trys recognized her right away and then Zach was attacking me." I paused a moment. "Trystan knew she was there before I did. Is that supposed to happen?"

My father waved the question away. "What else?"

I blushed.

"Don't worry about shocking me or embarrassing yourself. The two of you have been bonded since the bloodkiss. It's difficult to explain what that entails but anything and everything that happens between you. There's an element of compulsion."

I latched onto that notion. "She told him he didn't have any choice in the matter; that I stole his free will. That everything he felt for me was not real. We had a fight about it."

"Well in that she's wrong."

"That's what I told him!" I felt vindicated. Because I wasn't a hundred percent certain I was right. I hoped I was because I wanted his feelings to be genuine. I was feeling a bit giddy.

"The compulsion isn't going to be on him, Jace." He came around and sat on the front edge of his desk. "It's going to be on you. It's very important that you take all of your pills. You cannot afford to miss a day. Not now."

"I don't understand."

"Something has happened. I don't know if it was the girl. The bite. The mark. There are just too many unknown factors. But it's sparked a fire in you."

"He bit me." I whispered.

My father stood up and stepped towards me. "What?"

"Trystan. We were … kissing and he bit me."

"Did he draw blood?"

I nodded.

"When?"

"This morning.   He grabbed me and..." I blushed again. "Then after we argued about what she said we did it again."

"And he bit you? Both times?"

I nodded.

"Did you feel the bite?"

I thought about it for a moment. "Nuh uh. We just sort of noticed it. My lips were red and he thought I had bit him. But it wasn't me. I mean I tasted his blood, but I didn't bite him."

"Are you certain?"

"Dad." I gave him a look like he had just asked me the stupidest question ever. "I think I would know."

My father looked away as if he were remembering something. "Dad, what is it?"

"I think Trystan..."

"He's going to turn?"

"Not exactly. At least not what you think. Sometimes when a marked one is bitten, which rarely happens because the mark repels other vampires, but on occasion it does happen." My father shook his head as if he'd gotten off track. "Physiologically, Trystan is the same. He's not going to turn. But the mark isn't dormant any longer.   Until now, the mark has had no affect on you. Either of you. It was just a scar, but now that it's been triggered, you're going to be drawn to it, to him.   Fortunately your pills will counterweigh any additional bloodlust, which is why you mustn't under any circumstance miss taking them.   I want you to carry them with you at all times."

I nodded, my mouth dry. My heart was pounding.

"The mark is going to draw you to him, Jace. You're going to feel a whole new affinity for him. An overwhelming need to be near him."

"Okay." I was around him all the time anyway. We were practically brothers, except for that whole lusting after each other.

"No. It's going to be difficult, Jace.   Almost as bad as a bloodlust.   Seeing him will be more difficult than you can imagine. Being close to him, his scent, his touch, it's going to be unbearable. I can't describe it exactly, because it's different for everyone. The problem is, because the mark has been triggered, Trystan is going to need you too."

"So she was right. He has no choice."

"That's not what I mean, Jace.   Trystan is going to need your blood."

I didn't realize I had sat forward, sitting on the edge of my chair.   I let out the breath I'd been holding and slumped back into the chair.   "My blood?"

My father nodded.

"What happens if...?"

The look on my father's face said it all.   "That's not something...."

"He could die?"   I couldn't even imagine the look on my face.

"It's not as bad as you think."

"Dad.   First seeing him is going to be unbearable, and second he needs my blood or he'll die.   How much worse can it get?"

My father smiled and I was baffled.   "I know, it sounds bad."

"Ya think?"

"Listen to me Jace."   He got down on his knee and grabbed me by my shoulders.   "You'll get through this.   It's not like you two aren't together every day anyway.   You've been together since you were three years old and if I know anything, it's that you'll be together for the rest of your lives."

"You don't know that."   I was suddenly tired, utterly exhausted.

"No.   You're right.   I don't know.   What I do know is that you love him.   And I know that he loves you.   It's as plain as day."   He grinned again.   "Just like your mother and I."

My father undid the top two buttons of his Oxford and pulled it open, revealing a small white scar along the ridge of his collarbone. It was barely visible.

My eyes widened. "Wait Mom. She...   But I thought you."

"It's a long story." I couldn't help but laugh as he ruffled the top of my head, like everything was perfectly fine again.   "Long story short, your mother saw me at a school dance and knew I was the one."   He did the whole quote thing with his fingers when he said 'the one'. "Anyway, one thing led to another. So yeah, I know it's not going to be as bad as you think." He stood back up and went back behind his desk. "As long as you keep taking your pills and are there for Trystan, everything will be just fine. Difficult but fine."

"Easy for you to say." I couldn't even imagine the conversation I was going to have to have with Trystan. He was going to kill me.

CHAPTER EIGHT

A Taste for Blood II

Jace

"Wait! What?" Trystan was incredulous.

I'd been trying to explain everything, but it didn't seem to be working out the way I'd imagined it. "I wish you'd just come back to the house and let my dad explain it. You're getting way too mad at me. "

"What's to explain?" He put up a finger. "First, I'm marked by one vampire…Second, …"

"Trys…"

"I know, I know, you didn't mean it." He said mockingly.

I wanted to strangle him.   "You're such a pain in the ass."

"How the hell am I the pain in ass?"

"You act like you're the only one who's being affected by this."

"You've been a vampire all your life!"   His frustration was making him yell. "I've been dealing with this shit for a week and I didn't even know the truth until yesterday.   And now… NOW I have to fucking drink your blood or I'LL DIE!"

I held up my hands. "I know, I know. Look at it this way. We can call it your freaky fetish." I grinned, but he was having none of it. "You know, cuz you said I have some freaky fet…" Trystan scowled at me. "Nevermind."   I sat down on Trystan's bed. I could only sigh at my own frustration.   I lay back watching the Christmas lights twinkling on his walls. I couldn't help but think, if our situations were reversed, I wouldn't mind in the least to feast off of Trystan for the rest of my life.

"What?"

"Huh?" Shit, did I say that out loud?

"You said, if our situations were reversed and then I couldn't hear what you were saying."

Trystan sat down next to me. The mattress didn't move at all, but I couldn't help but turn towards him. Heat was rolling off of him in waves and I hesitantly laid a hand on his thigh. There was no sudden flush or orgasmic explosion at the contact; no excruciating unbearable agony. The way my father had described it, I was expecting to be racked with pain.

"What are we going to do?" His voice was bleak, broken.

I pulled him down by his hoodie, so that he was lying next to me, both of us staring at the ceiling. I twined my fingers with his, the fabric of his hoodie warm against my arm. "What can we do?" I don't think my voice sounded any less bleak. It was a miserable question. I was miserable. Even with Trystan beside me. "I don't like it when you're mad at me."

"I'm not mad at you." He didn't look at me when he said it. He just pulled the hood back up over his head.

"Feels like it." I said at the ceiling. "Will you come over? Let my dad explain everything. "

"Ok. But not tonight. I don't think I can take any more."

"What you wanna do then?"

He let go of my hand and jammed his deep into the pockets of his hoodie and sorta rolled over on his side so that he could look at me. The hoodie had pushed his hair flat and his bangs covered one of his eyes while the other peeked out at me. He had the cutest smile. "Hmm. I'm thinking I need junk food and crap TV. Oh! I know. Let's rent Mean Girls from Groovy Movies. And go to the Frozen Toad. Then on the way home we can drive thru Taco Bell." He paused for a moment. "One of the guys that works there is cute."

"Huh?"

"At Groovy Movies." He said nonchalantly.

"Are you trying to make me jealous."

Trystan smiled at that, then rolled back onto his back. "No, I'm just saying." He paused again. "I think his name is Billy. He's dating this guy named Ethan. Still, he's really cute."

"Okay. Okay. Okay" What the hell! "We've known each other for 14 years and you pick right now to tell me that you find some other guy hot?"

"First off, I said he was cute. Not hot. There's a difference. And Second, you've been dating girls for as long as I can remember and until I kissed you I had no idea you liked guys, much less me." He sat up then and turned around and looked down at me. "As a matter of fact, Jace Blackwell, I still don't know if you like me. SO if you're jealous…"

"I didn't say I was jealous." I tried not to sound pouty. "I asked if you were trying to make me jealous." I grabbed one of the strings to his hoodie and pulled on it. Trystan leaned away from me and his hoodie started to cinch closed around his face.

"Let go." He whined.

"Then come here." I pulled on the string again and this time he fell on top of me. His weight felt so comfortable, so right. I struggled to pull his hands from his pockets as I rolled us both over until I straddled him and his hands were pressed against the mattress. I leaned down over him, our lips inches apart. "Don't make me jealous. I can't bear that."

"Oh yeah?" His eyes twinkled mischievously. "Serves you right."

I started to lean down to kiss him but stopped myself. "No biting." I said, then kissed him. A quick tentative kiss. His lips were soft, softer than I remember. But our first two kisses were hungrier. I took another quick kiss. "And by the way, I told you after you kissed me the first time how I felt." Another kiss, this time a longer one. He pushed his hips up against me and wrapped a leg around me. I almost laughed when he moaned into my kiss. I pulled back and looked at him, felt his chest rising and falling with each deep breath. "As I recall, you called me a jerk and an asstard." I hopped up. Looking down at Trystan, I couldn't help but laugh at the expression on his face. "Okay. Let's go."

"What?" Trys was confused.

"Frozen Toad. Taco Bell. Oh and we have to rent Mean Girls from your boyfriend."

"You're doing this on purpose. Cuz I made you jealous." Trys crossed his arms over his chest and pouted. It took a great deal of will power not to jump right back on top of him.

"Serves you right."

Trystan stuck his tongue out at me and reluctantly got up off the bed. I pretended not to notice as he adjusted himself.

Our ride to the Frozen Toad was quiet although when he took my hand in the car I mentally bellowed gleefully at the top of my lungs. His hand was warm as he played his thumb along the ridge of my knuckles. I looked at him for the briefest of moments and then straight-ahead. "Trys? Do you really love me?"

"I've never loved anybody else."

I laughed nervously. I really didn't know how to react to that. "Why?"

His voice was a hushed whisper. "You're like my brother, my soul mate, my best friend all rolled into one person." He scrunched up his face. "Wait, ewww, not my brother." He let go of my hand then and looked out the window. "Except. I don't know now. I mean, I want to be in love with you. But I don't know if that's what I'm feeling. I mean you're my best friend. You saved my life, even though I didn't really know that until…" He turned back towards me, tucking one leg under him, his expression determined. "I don't know what love is, Jace. With you, I mean. You've been there as long as I can remember. And I've loved you for I don't know how long. And I've dreamed of you loving me, kissing me and now…the circumstances are a little fucked up."

There was a ton of people in the parking lot, music blaring from speakers through open car windows, a couple of jocks tossing a football back and forth and a gaggle of cheerleaders just out of the video store bunched in the middle one of the parking spots closest to the restaurant; everything seemed so normal.

I pulled into a spot and cut the engine. Trystan reached for the door handle and stopped, leaning back in the seat. "What you said about not being able to bear it if I made you jealous…you've dated 11 girls since I've known you and every time, every time I felt like I was dying." He started to say something else but then just nodded to himself and then got out of the car.

I sat there a moment, the engine ticking as it cooled.   I watched him lingering at the front of the car, waiting for me, his hands buried deep in his pockets, the hoodie pulled tight around him.   He looked back at me and jumped up and down. "Hurry up. It's coooooold."

We sat in the corner, eating our ice cream. I absently dug at a chunk of fudge with my red plastic spoon. I didn't understand why they used such small spoons. It really didn't change how I ate my ice cream in giant globs. I looked up and caught Trys staring at me.   "Wha?" I asked around a mouthful of double chocolate fudge.

He shook his head, smiling. "Nothing."

I swallowed and nudged him with my foot. "What?" I asked with a whine.

"This is just surreal." Trys held the spoon in front of him, licking it like a lollypop.   I wasn't certain if he was trying to be provocative, but watching him, his tongue, those lips and the way he returned my gaze, I felt a sudden stirring in the pit of my stomach. I was suddenly very warm and acutely aware of everything in my surroundings; the incredible amount of Aquanet the elderly woman in the booth across the aisle was wearing on her hair as well as the severe halitosis she had to endure from her husband, not to mention his abnormal heart rhythm. Two booths down, the blonde cheerleader with the lazy eye staring off in two directions was going through that special time of the month and her boyfriend of seven months was cheating on her with the brunette who sat across the table from them. The snarky girl behind the counter, who had taken their order and prepared their sundaes, was releasing a plume of pheromones in reaction to Aaron Guthrie; the school quarterback.

"Earth to Blackwell, come in Blackwell." Trys waved his hands in front of me.

"Huh." The scents coming off of Trystan were innumerable. His cologne, which he put on yesterday, the bodywash, which was clearly his mother's, a hint of body odor, musky and titillating, the laundry detergent from his freshly washed hoodie, and a subtle yet obvious scent of cum. "We gotta go!" I stood up and reached across the table and grabbed his hand. The sensation that surged through me in that moment was an explosion, knocking me back into my seat. I jerked my hand away from him. I remember when we were little Trystan and I stuck our tongues in between the terminals of a nine-volt battery. The feeling was similar to that only now my arm was numb to my shoulder.

"What's the matter?" I could actually smell Trystan's concern.

I shook my head. I didn't tell Trystan everything about what my father had said; about how difficult it was going to be for me. I watched him get up and sit down next to me. His fingers slid down my arm and it felt like fire. I arched my back; my knee jerking up and kicking the table, jangling the dishes along with the salt and peppershakers and the ceramic sugar packet holder. I shrugged away from his touch, taking a slow deep breath. I looked over at Trys. "Water. I need water."

I watched Trys run up to the counter. I reached into my pocket and pulled out the mint tin I carried my pills in. I was chanting in my head a whole mind over matter mantra to fight the innate urges roiling to the surface. I felt the bloodlust surging and my fangs pricking like two syringes. Ignoring the curious stares, I ran to the bathroom, lunging into the first stall and falling to my knees.

"Jace? Jace! What the hell?" The bathroom door slammed against the wall as Trystan entered.

I vomited up the ice cream. I looked back over my shoulder with pleading eyes as he stood in the stall entry. "Trys, you gotta leave."

Trys shook his head. "No. Tell me what to do."

"Run!" I bellowed it, my throat raw, my muscles taut as I gripped the cold porcelain toilet and vomited again.

"Jace."

I reached into my pocket and grabbed my keys and threw them at him. "Go! I'll be fine. But I need you to go. Now."

He took a step towards me and I flew at him, slamming us both against the blue-tiled wall behind him. I had a firm grip on his throat. In an instant I could feel his pulse, taste his fear and at the same time it felt like an electric current pulsed through me. "Fuck!" I jerked away from him, crashing into the stall door and slipping to the floor. The repellent odor of piss and shit overwhelmed me and I suffered a bout of dry heaves. "Trys. Please. Go." I battled with each word. I started shaking, gripping the base of the bathroom stall; the whole stall shook with me. I watched him back pedal away from me slowly. I don't know what I looked like; wild, crazed, an animal, but I could see the look in Trys' eyes and that look ripped through me. The anguish I suffered was like nothing I'd ever felt, as if the air I breathed was flame and the tears running down my face were acid. My very soul shrieked in agony. It was only after Trys had left that I was overcome by a blissful blackness that engulfed me.

CHAPTER NINE

A Taste for Blood III

Trystan

I woke up completely disoriented. Jace's bed was one of my favorite places. Not for the reason you might think. I stretched wincing at the pain in my shoulder. We had hit the bathroom wall pretty hard. I sat up and looked over at the cot Jace's mother had made up for me. I remembered going to sleep on it, but couldn't recall when I moved from the cot to Jace's bed. I drew the goose-down comforter over my shoulders and burrowed deeper into their warmth, inhaling Jace's familiar scent. It was only then that it occurred to me that Jace wasn't with me. I jerked up and scanned the room again, my heart beating wildly. I could still see the look in his eyes, feral, predatory, and hungry. I put a hand to my throat. I could feel raised tender flesh where he had gripped me by the throat.

"Jace." I whispered. "Where are you?"

Jace opened the door to his bedroom and peeked in at me. He seemed perfectly normal. "Want some toast?"

I flung the blankets off and ran to the door and threw myself at him. He wrapped his arms around me and I heard him shudder at the contact but he tightened his embrace for a moment before letting go.

"Are you alright?" I didn't give him any time to respond. "You scared the shit out of me!" I shoved him against the wall. "Fucker. Don't smile at me like that. What the hell?"

Jace looked down at his hands. "I left a few things out."

"Ya think!" I plopped back down on Jace's bed.

"Nice undies by the way."

I looked up at him and then down at myself.   Jace was fully clothed so it didn't occur to me that I wouldn't be.   I wore a pair of black and yellow Batman briefs I found at Wal-Mart.   They were cute as hell.   I pulled the comforter over me, embarrassed.

"There was blood."

The color drained from Jace's face. "Trys, I'm sorry."

"It's okay." I rubbed my throat.   "Your parents and I had 'the talk.'"

"I should have told you."

"Told me that I make you, as your father put it, libidinous." I couldn't help but smirk at his discomfort.

"Shut   up.   Technically   it's   the   mark   that   makes me...libidinous."

"Ohhhh. Technically is it?" I stood up, letting the comforter fall away.

Jace's eyes rounded. "You're bad. Bad! My parents are right down stairs. Mom's making you toast! Bad!"

"Mmmm.   Toast." I stepped into my jeans. Jace didn't look away until I popped my head through the top of my BOTDF T-shirt.

"Bad."   He muttered to himself.   He had taken a step towards me but had a white knuckled grip on the doorknob.

"Okay. I'm sorry. Breathe."

He pinched his eyes closed and took a big calming breath.

"What happened to you last night?"

Jace shook his head.   "I remember you leaving.   The next thing I remember is Dad waking me up.   I was in the woods, by our tree."

His expression was pained and serious. "It hurt so much. I..." He shook his head. "Anyway. Mom's sacrificing a loaf of bread in your honor." His smile was half hearted and strained.

"Jace, what is it? And don't tell me nothing.   Last time you held out on me, you ended up almost eating me."   I exaggerated, trying to bring a little levity but it didn't work.

"I don't remember what happened after you left. I lost like 6 hours. What if I ended up hurting someone? Or worse."

"You didn't."

"You don't know that! I don't know that. You said yourself I almost..." Jace sat down next to me, his hands held in front of him between his knees.

"Jace, I was kidding."

"Trys, I was in the middle of a bloodrage. Dad kept on asking me to remember. But I couldn't. He seemed worried. Like he knew something but wasn't telling me." He started to reach for my hand but stopped himself.

"Your dad has never kept anything from you before. Why would he start now?" I reached behind us and grabbed his comforter, yanking the corner from under his butt and then draped it over his shoulders. I wrapped my arms around him, looking to make sure none of me was touching any of him. "If he thought you needed to know, he'd tell you and when the time comes I'm sure he will, if there's anything to tell." I pulled the comforter up over his head and plopped a half dozen innocent kisses all over the vicinity of his face. "Now bring me to my toast."

I was on my third helping of toast when Jace's father came into the kitchen. He stood between Jace and I, clapping us both on the shoulders. "How are my boys this morning?"

I made happy jovial noises in between bites of toast.

"You remember anything else? He was looking at Jace who shook his head in response.

"You know I spoke with Trystan last night?" Jace's father squeezed my shoulder affectionately.

"Yeah, he told me you had 'the talk'"

His father laughed at that. "The talk?" There was a swollen pause before he asked; "I don't need to have the talk with you two, do I? I mean you don't have to worry about getting preg..."

I choked on my toast.

"Dad! Seriously? First thing in the morning? I think we have more important things to talk about other than sex. Which, we haven't had, by the way." Jace dropped his face into his hands.

Jace's father tapped me on the back.

"I'm alright." I coughed and reached for my glass of milk. I knew my face and ears were a brilliant crimson.

"Seriously, before your mother comes back, if there's anything you need to talk about…in that area…"

"Oh my God." Jace was blushing furiously. "Dad. We're good."

He gave us paternal hugs. "Just doin' my job, ya know." He gave his super dad pose; chest out, balled fists on his hips as he looked out at an imaginary job well done.

Jace rolled his eyes. "So embarrassing."

I loved his parents. Don't get me wrong I loved my mother more than anything in the world, but she was over protective, trying to keep me safe from the big bad world. The idea of having a conversation with her about sex with Jace was mortifying.

"Okay. We're going to start from the beginning; the very beginning." His earlier mirth was gone, replaced with a strained gravity.

We went through the story recalling the events of the last week. Jace's father inserted questions, seemingly insignificant, our answers equally trivial. He focused a great deal of attention on the mystery girl.

"You'd never seen her before Monday?"

I shook my head but felt a persistent nagging familiarity about her that I couldn't rationalize with words.

"What is it?" Both Jace and his father were looking at me.

"Huh?"

"You looked like you wanted to say something."

"No…Well…It's just, there's something about her. I keep thinking she looks familiar. That's not some sorta vampire hoodoo to make me more trusting and stuff, is it?"

Both Mr. Blackwell and Jace looked at me liked I'd just grown a third eye in the middle of my forehead.

"Some sort of vampire hoodoo?" Jace leaned over and thumped me in the forehead. "Seriously? You're what give vampires a bad name."

I couldn't help but laugh. It started out as a little smirk but then it was a full-throated laugh. "Give vampires a bad name. Oh my god. That is like the last thing I would ever expect to hear when the person saying it is completely and totally sincere.

Mr. Blackwell on the other hand wasn't the least bit amused. At first I thought it was with Jace or me. "Jace...son, I've been a little remiss when it comes to explaining our existence. Your mother and I, like any good parent, just wanted to keep you sheltered from certain elements."

"What's that supposed to mean, certain elements?" Jace sat at one of the other barstools and looked at his father.

"It was for the best. The chances of any sort of encounter...well we certainly didn't expect...our circumstances here are rather..."

"Dad! A complete sentence would be nice."

"We've never had reason to tell you everything."

"Dad. You're starting to freak me out."

"Boys..." The toaster interrupted him.

I looked up abashed. "What? I'm a stress eater."

"Let's go into the library." Mr. Blackwell gave me a look that said in no uncertain terms was I permitted to bring my toast. I'm not ashamed to say, I crammed the whole thing in my mouth and vacuumed the crumbs up like a Hoover.

"Wha?"

"Neanderthal." Jace shook his head as he followed his father.

The library was my favorite place in the whole house. Three of the four walls were lined with floor to ceiling bookshelves of dark mahogany. Eight-foot French doors framed by double bookshelves covered the fourth wall. A series of inset skylights illuminated the room naturally. Dust motes in the slanting sunlight and the subtle scent of warm wood made the library a captivating sanctuary. Jace and I plopped down on the plush leather sofa while Jace's father went over to the far wall behind two matching leather chairs. He started to pull out a book but apparently it was a release for a secret lever. There was a muted click and Jace's father spun a portion of the bookshelf, revealing a hidden set of books.

"Okay, when I said you were freaking me out. Really. You're freaking me out." We both got up and slowly walked towards Jace's father. Jace had taken my hand, first hesitantly but as we drew near, his grip tightened. While I felt a comfort that I knew he was hoping for, still I wondered at the pain he must be feeling.

His father had pulled a book from the shelf. It looked old, bound in leather and embossed in gilded lettering; the words foreign, the lettering not even in the English alphabet.

ЛегендеиЛореоф тхе Вампире

Mr. Blackwell traced his fingers along the lettering as he read. "The Legends and Lore of the Vampire. A great deal of it is nonsense, of course, but certain things are true. And had I read this before your mother gotten pregnant the first time..."

"The first time? What are you talking about?"

I squeezed Jace's hand for support but he was oblivious of me and stared at his father.

"Your mother and I... You know her parents died shortly after we met. We were young...younger than you two and while she knew what she was, there was a great deal she was not told. Before they could tell her, the fire..."

"I don't... What does this have to do with anything?"

"You had a sister." Mr. Blackwell sighed. "You have a sister."

"What?"

Mr. Blackwell looked at the book, opening it carefully, scanning the pages slowly. Then he looked up at Jace. "We didn't know. Until it was too late."

"Until what was too late?"

"Vampire infants are stillborn." There was anger in his voice, anger and sadness. " We didn't know where to go. We weren't aware of the network for our kind. By the time we found out..." He threw the book down with such ferocity, I stepped back. I tried to let go of Jace's hand but he had a vice-like grip.

"You think this girl is my sister? That she's your daughter? But how could she be...I mean if she was stillborn."

"Someone must have known who we were, what we were. Someone who knew enough to take your sister, to keep her alive."

"But how?"

"I don't know." He looked out the doors, muttering to himself. "The umbilical vein carries blood. There would be enough..." He shook his head and turned back towards us. "Nothing to your mother about this."

"But.."

"Jace, if I'm wrong..."

"If you're right, mom has a right to know." Jace countered.

"Once we know for certain; I'll tell her. Until then, I will not hurt your mother with false hopes. If I'm right, she'll be devastated. I'll not take the chance and then be wrong."

I looked at Jace's father and then at Jace. They had the same features, their eye shape, their jawlines, hair color, but Jace had his mother's lips. They were full, while his father's were narrow. Jace also had his mother's lithe frame. I closed my eyes and recalled the mystery girl. The one thing that leapt out at me was my unwitting association of her to Jace, both in the moment and in my dream. But on second thought, recalling her, the familiarity was unmistakable.

Jace had a sister.

CHAPTER TEN

Commitments

Trystan

"I made your favorite." My mother prided herself in her cooking. She loved to cook. And as far as she was concerned, everything was my favorite.   My mother put down a platter of pancakes and bacon then pressed a hand to my forehead "Are you feeling okay? You look a little pale. And you feel a little warm."

"I'm just tired.   It's been a long week."   That was an understatement.

"Let me get you some juice. Vitamin C is what you need." She grabbed my face in both hands inspecting me, turning my face this way and that.

"Mom, I'm fine." I leaned back out of her grasp, weaving around her and forking 4 pancakes onto my plate. I crammed a whole slice of fried bacon into my mouth. "Where's the syrup?" The bacon was melt in your mouth perfection. I grabbed three more slices, while eating another one before my mother returned with the syrup and orange juice.   I was starving.

"Well at least your appetite is fine."

My mother wasn't an eater, but rather more like a mama bird and her baby bird. I think if she thought she could get away with it, she'd regurgitate food just to feed me. I winced at the image.

I couldn't help but think of Jace. 24 hours ago he was an only child and now, if his father was right, he had an older sister. Of course, it was only a week ago that I had a crush on my normal everyday run of the mill best friend and now he's my vampire boyfriend. I blushed at that thought.

After procuring promises from Jace and I about not saying anything to anyone about anything, Mr. Blackwell sent us on our way. We ended up on Jace's bed, him on one corner, me on the other, playing Xbox.

My trigger finger was working over time to the point of cramping. "So…"

"What?" His mouth was quirked, his eyes squinted, as he leaned forward into the game, his grip on the controller, white knuckled, such was his concentration.

"What are we doing?"

He continued to play, my question pretty much ignored, acknowledged, but ignored. I'm pretty sure he was thinking the same thing. Sure the obvious, playing video games, blasting the hell out of marauding zombies. We were actually working our way through a list of the top ten zombie games for Xbox. This one was a bit lame in comparison to the big name zombie titles but still; it met the criteria, killing zombies. He gestured towards the television with his controller and shrugged his shoulders like the answer was the most obvious thing in the world.

I dropped my controller and looked at him. "You know what I'm talking about."

Jace rolled his head, easing the tension in his shoulders. "Do we have to talk about this now. It's been a shit week. For both of us. I just want to kill some zombies."

He turned back towards the television only to watch his player get mauled by a zombie. He pounded the buttons on his controller, his tongue sticking out, and then slammed it down on the bed. "Son of a bitch." The screen was suddenly covered with splotches of virtual gore and blood.

"Now can we talk?"

His look of disdain was almost comical. "About what?"

"You and me."   I reached over and slugged him. "I can't believe you just rolled your eyes."

He laughed, rubbing his arm.   "We're not gonna have to do couples counseling, are we?"

"You're an ass."

"I've heard."   His tone was dismissive.

"Fine. Forget it."

"No no… by all means, let's talk about it."

"Fuck you, Jace Blackwell." I looked for something to throw at him.   Finding nothing, I lunged at him, knocking both of us off the bed. I could tell he was trying not to laugh. His hoodie protected him from any direct contact. I was pissed which is why I leaned down and licked his neck. He arched his back in response and his eyes were pained.

"What was that for?"

"For patronizing me." I leaned down and licked him again.

"Okay. Okay. Shit!"

I grinned, trying not to look smug.

"That fucking hurts.   Asshole!" He rubbed at his neck with his shoulder.

I still had his wrists pinned. He thrust his hips up, trying to knock me off of him.   I couldn't help but smile. "Are we gonna talk, now?" I leaned in to lick him again.

"Yes!   Yes.   Just quit that!"   I could tell he wasn't really hurting too bad. He struggled halfheartedly, a smirk on his face. "Get off me."

"But I like it here."   He was suddenly blushing.   I was perched on his crotch, the pain from my licks a distraction from his apparent arousal.

"You are cruel. Cruel! Cruel! Cruel!"   His thrusts became involuntary and I pushed back to meet them.

"Trys, you gotta get off." He flung me off effortlessly.   He began to writhe, turned on his side, curling into a fetal position, his breathing heavy, his fists balled, muscles taut, eyes squeezed shut.

"Oh shit. Not again." My hands floated above him. I dared not touch him, no matter how much I wanted.

"My pills." His voice was strained. He gestured blindly. "Backpack."

I stood up and looked around his room. Dirty clothes lay scattered everywhere. I saw his backpack in the corner. I dug through it frantically; unzipping the separate compartments and dumping the contents on the floor. I grabbed the mint tin and was back by his side. He was breathing heavy, but his muscles appeared relaxed and not straining against some invisible bond.

"I'm gonna go get your dad."

"No." He grabbed my shirt. "I'm fine. I just need the pills." He looked at me, smiling wryly. "You're just gonna have to quit doing that."

I blushed. "Sorry."

"Trys. I'm teasing." He pulled me down and kissed me and while I was careful not to touch his skin, he kissed me hungrily. "Be my boyfriend."

I pulled back away from him. He smiled and I nearly melted. "What?"

"I said. Be. My. Boyfriend." Each word was punctuated by a kiss.

"What's wrong with you? Take your pills. You're delirious." I laughed.

"I'm serious Trys." It felt like he was looking deep into my soul. "You said you wanted to talk about us, about you and me. There is no me without you. Be my boyfriend."

My answer, of course, was a resounding yes. I pounced on him, kissing him all over his face. When I pulled back he had a wretched albeit adorable smile on his face. "Oh shit. I'm sorry."

Jace laughed. I plopped down next to him, my fingers caressing the sleeve of his hoodie.

"What are you thinking?" My mother rapped her knuckles on the table.

I nearly choked on my bacon. "Huh?"

"I asked, what were you thinking?"

"Nothing. Just homework."

My mother looked at me; like mother's do. She shook her head, seeing through the lie. "Okay. We'll call it homework.

Though I've never seen anyone smile at the notion of homework."

I crammed a forkful of pancakes into my mouth and shrugged haplessly at being unable to respond.

"How's Jace?" She sipped her coffee, watching me over the rim of her cup.

"He's fine." I could play nonchalant.

"Good. Good." She nodded and took a small bite out of her raisin bread. "I haven't seen him lately."

"He's been busy." I reached across the table for more bacon. My mother nudged the platter closer. I contemplated more pancakes. "He's picking me up this morning for school."

"Oh really? That's good." My mother smiled, knowingly.

"Uh huh." I plated two more pancakes and drowned them in syrup. I dipped a slice of bacon into the syrup and wolfed it down. My stomach growled.

"Didn't you eat yesterday?"

"Yeah. I had a pizza. And some toast. Why?"

"You act like you're starving to death."

I hesitated a moment, the forkful of pancakes halfway to my mouth. I rolled my eyes. "I'm just hungry this morning. A growing boy." I stuffed the pancakes in my mouth then patted my tummy, which was surprisingly flat considering how much I'd eaten in the last 24 hours.

"Okay." She got up and ruffled my hair as she walked past and into the kitchen. "You want me to pack you a lunch?"

"Whatever." I grabbed another piece of bacon. "We'll probably just go somewhere and eat." I said between bites.

"I have bookclub tonight, so I won't be here when you get home. I'll make something and put it in the oven to keep it warm." I could see her in my mind's eye, standing in front of the open refrigerator, deciding what she was going to make for dinner. "You want chicken or spaghetti?"

"Whatever you make is fine. I'll eat it." There wasn't much I wouldn't eat. There was the evil vegetable triumvirate of okra, raw tomatoes and hominy that gave me an automatic gag response. No American cheese, either; that stuff was gelatinous evil. Everything else was fair game.

"I think I'll make spaghetti." She called back. "You want garlic bread. I can make garlic bread, I know you like that cheesy garlic bread."

My stomach growled again. I almost laughed out loud. Garlic and vampires don't mix.

I heard Jace's car in the driveway. I listened for the front door to open. "Mom. Jace is here. We're about to leave."

"Okay. Tell Jace he's welcome to dinner."

I rolled my eyes. "He knows mom. You tell him every time you see him."

"Okay. Okay." She pushed the kitchen door open. "Tell him anyway. And don't roll your eyes at me. It's rude."

I slung my backpack over my shoulder. "Fine."

"And don't, fine me, either."

The front door opened. "Trys! Let's go."

I crammed the last piece of bacon in my mouth and gave my mother a quick kiss on the cheek. "Have fun at bookclub."

She patted the top of my head and then gave me a little shove towards the door. "Get."

Jace had left the door ajar and gone back to his car. He really didn't drive all that much. He wasn't a big fan and drove like an old lady. That's why I mostly drove.

"Mom said to come to dinner tonight." I watched him fiddle with the rearview mirror and sit up straight in his seat, before starting the ignition. I propped my knees on the dashboard. "We're having spaghetti."

"Okay." He looked over his shoulder, both of them.

"I don't mind driving." He was making me nervous.

"It's okay. I'm fine."

"You don't seem fine. You seem jittery. Like too much coffee jittery."

"I told dad about last night; about the attack. He made me take double dose this morning. It's not supposed to hurt me. But..." He held out his hand. The tremor was obvious. "My whole system is in overdrive." I heard him sniff. I looked at him.

"Oh my god! Jace...your nose. It's bleeding." I unbuckled and looked in the glove compartment for a tissue but before I could react any further the scent of his blood hit me. It felt like a sledgehammer to the gut. I wailed and fought the urge to throw up. I clawed at the door handle and pushed the door open with my shoulder. I fell out of the car onto my hands and knees and vomited. I felt Jace's hand on my back. He rubbed up and down, consoling me in a whisper. "It's gonna be okay." He pulled me into his arms my head resting on his chest. He shoved up the sleeve of his sweater and held his wrist in front of me, I watched as he pressed a thumbnail into the soft flesh of his wrist. He grimaced as a thin line of blood trailed down his arm to his elbow. "Here."

I knew what he wanted me to do. I shook my head, burying my face in the warmth of his sweater."

"Trys." I peered up at him. His eyes were pained. "You have to do it."

I took his wrist and felt him jerk at the contact.

"It's okay." He reassured me, breathlessly.

All I heard was him; his heavy breathing as my lips touched his wrist, then a mewling cry as I began to drink. I drank, satisfying a craving I'd never experienced before. I was ravenous. His hushed cry became a wailing howl as I quenched my thirst. He tried to pull free but I held on, unwilling to release him. He pushed at me, first gently then shoved hard, propelling me against the car.

Both of us were breathing heavily. Contrary to my expectation, Jace appeared perfectly fine. His eyes were vibrant, his pallor, ruddy.

I sat up, feeling so alive.

CHAPTER ELEVEN

Commitments II

"He's protected." The girl's voice was muted and tentative.

"That is easily remedied."

She shook her head. "I won't do it."

"The Blackwells and their ilk have too long been blind to the sins of their past and it is high time they paid for them. "

"I'm a Blackwell."

"Yes, but in name only."   The man leaned back in the leather chair, relishing the opulence he had made for himself. "I have raised you as my own, against the wishes of my own. When the time comes, when all is right, you will take him and make him ours. I wouldn't ask you to spill your own blood." He looked out the window. "I have others for vengeance."

She nodded her understanding.

A mewling cry came from the corner. They both looked at Zachary Holt.

"You should not have made him. You are not ready." The man rose from his seat and strode purposefully to the boy, watching as he scrambled back. His once vital flesh was sallow, his eyes sunken, his body trembling. What little blood that remained in him had blackened.   The putrid scent of death surrounded him.   The man raised a hand in the direction of the girl. "You made a commitment to take care of your own, just as I have to take care of mine. Come." He beckoned her closer. "In this, I will instruct you." She took his hand.   "There is darkness in life for our kind." He shook his head saddened. He pulled a long silver blade from a scabbard affixed to the wall. It caught the evening sunlight reflecting golden shafts. "It is our way." With some ceremony, he carefully offered the blade to the girl. She looked at it and then to the man.

"I can't." She tried to refuse the blade but the man insisted.

"You must steel your heart. He will not die. He is an abomination of your making who will continue to wither and suffer. You must take care of your own." He gestured at the blade and then turned his back on her as she slipped her hand through the ivory hilt and grasped the sword.

"We must fulfill the covenant." He nodded to himself as he strode back to his seat. "There are those who blaspheme the will of the Blood, deny the rites that redeem us, deny the true way. They are heretics. They strive to destroy the old ways."

He smiled as he heard the blade whistle through the air and the boy's terrified shriek cut short. The blade clattered to the floor and he listened as her footsteps carried her from his den.

Jace

We were both sitting in the library, Trystan on the leather sofa, me on the floor in front of him, between his knees, my back to him. I could feel his fingers play along my back as he read over my shoulder. We had retrieved the old books from the hidden shelves and were currently reading The Ancestral Lines of Blood.

"I forgot that Blackwell is your mother's name." Trys put his chin on my shoulder and I could feel his breath teasing the hairs on my neck.

"Yeah. She was the one with the Blood. Dad was just like you."

Trystan laughed. "Like muggles."

I rolled my eyes. Although in essence it was true.   Still, Harry Potter references applicable to my life seemed farfetched and surreal.

The Blackwell bloodline stretched back 700 years in a matriarchal line. With no daughter, until a week ago, I had been the last of the line.

Trystan reached for a blue leather tome, The Immortal Dead Fallacy. I hissed as his arm barely slipped across the back of my neck.

"Sorry. Sorry." He made to kiss my neck but I shied away. He settled for kissing the top of my shoulder, which was safely covered with a t-shirt. I reached for my tin of pills and plucked out two and washed them down with my Dr. Pepper. I offered the bottle to Trystan who never turned away Dr. Pepper.

"Okay." He took a quick drink then handed the bottle back. "Somewhere in all of these books there has to be a Kama Sutra for Vampires and the Marked Ones They Love." He looked at me. "Your parents did have sex, didn't they?"

"No I'm the product of immaculate conception. No wait.... I'm the original Cabbage Patch doll, yup born in Babyland General Hospital. No wait..."

"Shut up." Trystan scowled.

"I was the third wish from an old genie's lamp my mother found at a garage sale."

"Smart ass." He hit me on the back of the head with his book.

I looked back over my shoulder with a smirk. "Ask a stupid question."

"There are no stupid questions."

I leaned on his denim-clad knee and laughed. "Oh babe, that's just something stupid people say."

Trystan lean forward and suddenly I felt a sting as he kissed the back of my neck.

"Shit! What in the hell was that for?" I rubbed my neck, scooting forward beyond his reach.

"You called me stupid." He smiled and opened the book, its gilded edges catching the soft light. He leaned back folding his legs under him and started reading.

"You're a little bitch."

His smile made my toes curl. "And don't you forget it, mister." Trystan blew me a kiss without looking up from the book.

We read for a good hour, not talking, the only sound were pages being turned and Trystan's stomach growling. It got to the point where I ran down stairs and brought up a tray of peanut butter and jelly sandwiches and a family size bag of Doritos.

I watched him as he ate. He ate ravenously.

"What?" Trystan looked up from the bag of chips, powdery orange cheese coated his fingertips. He licked them absently. He upended the bag and I heard the last of the chips slide into his mouth. He held his hand out for my Dr. Pepper. I rolled my eyes as he drank the last of it.

He gestured towards the book he'd been reading. "So according to this, you can live forever. You're immortal?"

I nodded. Immortality had certain inaccurate connotations.

"So where's the rest of the Blackwell clan?" He unfolded his legs and leaned towards me.

I could almost hear my father's voice when I spoke. "Immortality is the ability to live forever. It doesn't mean we are invulnerable to death." My father had gone into scientific detail; the biological process of cellular transdifferentiation. He had difficulty with layman's terms, which often times left me clueless or bored beyond comprehension. I wasn't about to attempt to explain it to Trystan. "Anyway, who wants to live forever?"

Trystan pressed his foot into my crotch. "I'd live forever with you."

"You're such a romantic." I rolled my eyes but grabbed his foot. I traced a finger over his sock and stopped just short of touching the flesh of his ankle then I touched him tentatively drawing my fingers over and around the ankle. He tried to pull his foot away but I held it firm, pressed against me. The pain coursed through my hand like a current. I grimaced, gritting my teeth, determined to endure it. I felt an inexplicable arousal.

"Jace. Stop." He pulled free of my grasp.

I cradled my hand, rocking back and forth, breathing deep calming breaths, trying to gain control over the pain. Slowly the pain subsided, drifting in and out like an outgoing tide. My eyes were closed but I felt Trystan kneel down next to me. "Forever?" I asked him, then leaned in and kissed him. I couldn't help myself. The kiss shocked me, the pain a sudden exquisite overwhelming flash of fire through my whole body.

It was the shortest of kisses as Trystan pulled away almost immediately. He couldn't wipe away my tears, not with his hands. He pulled off his shirt and dabbed at my cheeks. "What's the matter with you?" He pushed me angrily. "Don't ever..." The sentence went unfinished. He leaned back against the couch. "We'll figure it out." He sighed. "We have to."

CHAPTER TWELVE

Commitments III

Trystan

"When I said, we'd figure it out..."

We looked ridiculous. And if someone walked in on us...well let's just say it looked like we were into something really kinky.

"What'd you tell your dad?" I was trying hard not to laugh.

"I just said we were going snorkeling in your pool." Jace pulled the neoprene sleeve as far down past his wrists as it would go. It was obvious, we'd both gone through a little growth spurt in the last year.

"And he believed you?" I smiled wryly. Certainly his father wasn't that obtuse.

Jace laughed out loud. "What do you think? He raised his eyebrows, then shrugged his shoulders like it was the most normal thing in the world to go snorkeling in winter. He had this smile on his face. Made me feel like a perv. But I wasn't about to tell him or wait around for a birds and the bees talk.

I mimicked Mr. Blackwell as I walked back from flipping the light switch off. "Physiologically, an erection is triggered by the parasympathetic division of the autonomic nervous system..."

"Would you shut up?" The halogen streetlights lit Jace's grin as he shoved me onto the bed.

"Oh my." He straddled me and I couldn't help but burst out laughing. "We must look absolutely absurd."

"Well, if you have a better idea..." He reached down, drawing his hand down my chest and tummy and stopped above my crotch. "...You know, where I can touch you, or...rub you."

I inhaled deeply at the sensation; friction and heat from the neoprene wetsuit and his hand teasing me.

The wetsuits were from Jace's family vacation the previous summer. It was supposed to be an educational vacation, snorkeling to view the destruction of the coral reefs, but in all honesty, the only thing I could pay attention to when Jace was in his wetsuit was Jace. It really left nothing to the imagination and took all my willpower to keep from educating Jace to my excitement. And let me tell you, an improperly adjusted hard-on is a terrible thing in a wetsuit. Neoprene doesn't have that much give.

"What?" Jace looked down at me.

"Huh?"

"You just have this look on your face like... I don't know. Like it hurts." His hand hovered just above my waist.

"I just remember the first time we wore our wetsuit down in the Caymans. We had to help each other. And every time you touched me and even worse, every time I touched. I wanted you so much. And believe me, it hurt."

"Oh yeah?" Jace had an evil smirk as he continued to stroke me through the suit, just sliding his hand up and down, the minute motion inside the suit: all I could do was moan in response.

"Oh my god, you gotta stop." I bucked and pulled him down beside me. "If I go too soon, I'm gonna be pissed."

Jace laughed. "Why?"

"Cuz I feel like a complete idiot." We were staring into each other's eyes. "And it took forever to get this damn thing on."

"Well if it makes you feel any better." He reached across the bed and tried to grope me but I pulled back.

"Wait! I swear to god Jace, if you make me cum. And don't make that pouty face." I flipped over on my other side and scooted back until Jace spooned me. "Why don't you go to town?"

"Talk about safe sex." He wrapped his arms around my waist pulling himself even tighter against me.

He got a little carried away and licked my ear lobe and growled in frustration. I imagine it was much like licking a 9 volt battery to him.

He tried to slip a hand lower, but I smacked it.

"Not yet."

"Fucker." Jace bit my shoulder softly. I could feel his teeth, even through the neoprene, just as I could feel how excited he was as he pressed tightly against me. He was pawing at my ass, his growling more adamant. I muffled laughter into my pillow as I pressed back. He bit me again. I couldn't help but wonder if vampires have a biting fetish. His grinding was becoming more fervent, his breathing deep and rhythmic; hot against my neck. His grip tightened around my waist. I moved his hand down. He responded immediately. While he couldn't grip me through the suit, still he worked his hand up and down. Whatever self-control he might have possessed disappeared. His grinding became a more enthusiastic banging, each thrust slamming against my backside followed by a throaty grunt. I wanted so much to turn around and kiss him, though to lose this little bit of contact seemed inconceivable. The friction inside the wetsuit was exquisite. I strained against my own reaction, trying to curl away from myself, but the suit kept everything rubbing forcefully against everything else and Jace's hand worked me until I could only cry out as I climaxed. Jace in turn slammed against me and I could only think that his orgasm was overwhelming because I felt his lips on the back of my neck, kissing over and over as he whispered my name.

Slowly his grip around my waist loosened. He stopped kissing abruptly, instead pressing his forehead against my back, his hands snaking up around my chest, hugging me tight. I hated the suits at that moment; more than anything, the lack of contact, that sensation of flesh on flesh, a need so innate, lost to us. I grabbed his sleeved arms and held them tight against my chest, my eyes cinched closed. I wanted his touch.

His bellow of frustration startled me. It was a roar of feral rage I felt. I looked back and saw for the first time, his fangs. They shone bright in the scant light, along with tears, which glistened in eyes that pierced my soul. He yelled out again and flung himself away from me, his arm flailing back and shattering the window. There was recognition in his eyes as he looked at me but also a hunger.

I wasn't frightened. Quite to the contrary, I felt an overwhelming craving of my own. A fire raged through me as I picked up the scent. Jace had cut himself on the glass. I stumbled back against the wall, doubled over as pain seared through me with each pulse of my heart. My gut clenched painfully. I shook my head, refusing to submit to the urge, the hunger.

"Trystan." His voice was so deep in his throat, it was almost unrecognizable. I looked up at him and he stood tall against the far wall but he offered his arm up, the neoprene sleeve sliced open, slick and shiny in the glow of the streetlight. I looked away, shaking my head. "Trystan!" He repeated himself forcefully, but said nothing else, as if it were the only word he knew. Another wave of pain coursed through me. My whimpering drew him as I slid down the wall. I knew I was crying, but only as an after thought, only after I felt him wipe the tears away. He cradled my head in his lap and the he fed me the first drops of his blood, dabbed from his fingers to my lips. "Trystan." This time Jace's hushed whisper enveloped me; took hold of me and carried me away into a welcome darkness.

CHAPTER THIRTEEN

A Quickening Pulse

Tristan

The moon was full, a huge bulbous yellow moon that glowed so bright over the forest that the winter trees cast stark shadows like black veins across my path.   The moonlight felt heavy on my back and those shadow branches were ropes tying me down.   Every step became more arduous, and it felt as though some of those shadows snapped and stung like rubber bands pulled too taut.   I dare not look back.   I heard the cracking of branches, and the wind whispered malignantly.   I could smell blood, the coppery scent filled my nostrils and coated my tongue and the moon was suddenly a filmy red that tinted everything crimson.   I looked back and regretted it immediately.   The shadows stretched towards me, slithering snakes rooted only in the darkness of the night.   I wanted to run but the air was suddenly gelatinous, holding me as darkness devoured the moonlight.   The wind howled ferociously; a whirlwind of screams buffeting me as I struggled to break free from the writhing shadows.   I recognize the silhouette of a single tree in the crimson glow of moonlight.   It stood tall, branches grasping at the bloody moon, as if to drag it from the heavens to the darkness of the earth.   I struggled towards the tree. The wind battered me, filled with a putrid scent of death that overwhelmed my senses, causing me to wretch.   The shadows thrashed out and bore into my skin, drawing a viscous black blood.

"Tristan." My name reverberated like a lone trumpet blast amidst a cacophony of chaos. I redoubled my efforts, scrabbling for every inch, kicking and clawing. I raged against the wind, my voice tearing painfully as I bellowed. The ground opened up and my rage became fear as I began sinking. The quicksand stank of blood and vomit and piss and shit and I found a new fervor to reach the tree. Something underneath grabbed at my foot. A skeletal hand rose before me, flesh clinging to it in rotted clumps. More and more bones rose to the surface. I sank further even as I scrabbled over skulls and fleshy decomposed body parts. I couldn't breathe; the very air thick and sluggish.

"Tristan!" Another trumpet blast; a rumbling thunderous wave that unbound me. I scrambled to my feet and ran. I reached a clearing, panting under a halo of white light. I looked around, shielding my eyes. The tree's trunk was colossal, bringing to mind the great redwoods in California. I peered up as I ran my hand along the coarse bark. I felt a pulse reverberating with my touch. A walked along the trunk's perimeter; feeling a steady thump-thump-thump through the thick bark. The further along I walked, the faster the pulse grew. I heard a muffled cry and raced forward watching the curve of the trunk, which seemed to go on forever. The cries grew stronger. I sprinted towards the cries, then stopped dead in my tracks.

They were both naked, their bodies covered in dirt, streaked with blood. Scratches were clawed into Jace's back. Jace looked back over his shoulder at me as he drove deep into the other boy. They groped at each other, flesh against flesh and Jace smiled diabolically, relishing in something we couldn't share. I felt a rage take over me as I watched Jace lean in for kiss after kiss, his eyes never leaving my face. I couldn't breathe and I was overcome with a cold sweat and everything was muted. I took a single step toward Jace, and instantly I was above him as he continued to fuck.

I struck out blindly. Jace was thrown back against the tree. He struck it and fell at the base seemingly unconscious. I looked down at the other boy. He tried scrambling away from me but had no traction in the leaves and branches, his naked feet skidding in the debris. I grabbed him by the leg and dragged him to the edge of the halo of light.   I forced him to his feet, ignoring the glistening tears as he attempted to free himself from my grasp.   Like with the tree, I felt the sudden thump-thump-thump of his heart.   It beat inside of me.   I looked at him, mystified.   I reached out and gently wiped his tears, cupping his cheek.   Relief filled his eyes.   It was only when my nails ripped into his throat that the relief vanished.   Hot blood gushed over my hand and wrist and I leaned in and drank.   Drank voraciously, each pulsing gush filling my mouth to overflowing. I felt it dripping down my chin and neck, soaking through my shirt.   I drank and his life pulse drowned out everything.   I felt his pulse weakening and a growl escaped me.   I bit hungrily into the flesh as I bore the weight of his body.   More blood pulsed as I opened a secondary artery.   I let him drop, his grip on my shoulder weak, his hand trailing down my blood-soaked shirt. Blood started pooling below his neck.   He looked up at me, his mouth working, trying to form words.   Nothing came forth but blood.   I sank to my knees and held his hand.   I leaned in and licked his lips, savoring the last trickle of his lifeblood.   I dropped his hand as I stood.

Jace leaned against the tree.   For a moment it appeared as though the tree and Jace were one, as if instead of leaning against the trunk, he was emerging from it.   He stepped towards me and touched me.   First tentatively, then he ripped at my clothes, tearing the blood-drenched fabric from my chest.   His nails slashed my chest but the wound disappeared quickly.   I felt nothing as he bit at me, his teeth sinking into my shoulder, into my chest.   I pulled him by the hair, pulling him straight back away from me, revealing his neck.   I felt my fangs piercing gums and in an instant I plunged them deep into Jace's neck.

"Jace!"   I woke with a start, breathing heavy, my heart hammering.   I looked around, disoriented, at first seeing nothing but darkness.   I kicked at the sheets and blankets then flung them off of me wiping frantically at my arms, kicking with my feet until I was free of them.   I felt grit under my feet, the grit of sand, of dirt.   And suddenly the smell of blood permeated the air.   I choked back the urge to vomit and clambered out of bed.   I raced to the bathroom.   My stomach clinched and I dry-heaved over the toilet.   My eyes watered and saliva flooded my mouth.

I heaved again, choking on nothing. I gasped for air as my stomach clinched tighter again and again. Behind closed eyes, I saw the tears of the boy. I could smell his fear. I could feel the weight of him as my dream self devoured his life force. I shook my head and hoisted myself up with the help of the counter and stared at myself in the mirror. My eyes were watery and bloodshot, my hair bedraggled, and my over-sized t-shirt wrinkled as if twisted. I sighed with relief, pressing my forehead against the cool mirror. I slapped the light switch off on my way out and the other on in my bedroom. I froze in my tracks. A pile of dirty clothes, ripped and blood-soaked, was in the corner below a smeared crimson handprint. I staggered back, conscious of the thump-thump-thump of my heartbeat.

CHAPTER FOURTEEN

A Quickening Pulse II

Jace

"Hey."

Trystan's scent filled the room, a cloud so rich and vibrant, it was dizzying. I turned and found him standing in the doorway to the library, a shaft of morning light illuminating him. I had to do a double take to make sure he was real and not a waking dream. He was stunning. His smile was subtle and alluring and blossomed as he realized I was admiring him. "You look good."

I got up on my knees on the couch and watched him take the few steps to me. "And you smell. Oh my God, what is that smell."

Trystan smelled one armpit and then the other. "What? Is it bad?"

I shook my head, closing my eyes. "No. No. No. But you need to stand over there." I pointed to the far wall by the staircase that led to the second floor. I got up and went to the French doors and opened them both wide, inhaling as deeply as I could.

"What's the matter?"

"I don't know. But you... You smell good enough to eat. And drink. And..." I adjusted myself and heard Trystan laugh nervously. I took several more gulps of fresh air. "Something's different. "

"What do you mean?" He asked hesitantly.

"Something about you is different." I strode with purpose to Trystan. He stared at me, blinking a couple of times as I leaned in closer. He appeared flawless: neither blemish nor imperfection marred his flesh, as if rejuvenated. I tried breathing through my mouth, his scent was so overwhelming, but the result was that I could taste him. I staggered back. My every instinct cried out for him. There was lust in that silent wail and hunger, an insatiable hunger that shook me. Trystan must have seen my reaction; that hunger, because he stepped back quickly, a fear blossoming in his eyes. I gripped the sofa back for stability, leaning on it, pressing myself against it, all the while yearning to throw myself at him.

I watched him drop his gaze, then stare up at me again, his lips parting as if he had something to say.

"What is it, Trys?"

"Something happened last night. I'm not quite sure what exactly. When I woke up, I thought it was a dream, a nightmare. There was blood in my room. And on the clothes. I thought it was…"

"Wait. What clothes…what are you talking about?" I could smell his hesitation, his uncertainty, and his fear.

"I thought it was a dream. But…but I think I killed…" He continued.

"Okay. Stop. You're gonna have to stop and start from the beginning. I'm lost."

Trystan took a deep breath and in a rush of words told me. He blushed at finding me in the forest as he put it, 'rutting like an animal' and I could smell his jealousy. He spoke quietly of killing the boy, devouring his lifeblood and whispered of plunging his fangs into my throat. I listened raptly. "I thought it was all a dream until I found the clothes and the blood."

I hadn't notice the trash bag on the floor by the entrance until Trystan went for it, picking it up with hesitation. He carried it to me, holding it at arms length, his expression distasteful.

I opened the bag and nearly retched. The reek of death and rot rose, an invisible plume engulfing me. Trystan stepped back, covering his nose. I lifted the shirt out of the bag, it was stiff, the blood a viscous black. I looked up at Trystan. "Describe him. The boy."

Trystan shook his head. "I dunno. I didn't recognize him. He was just someone you were fucking."

I fought to keep from grinning. "Well, that part was definitely a dream. I think I would have remembered that."

Trystan frowned and gave me the finger. "Not funny." He grinned half-heartedly. He nodded towards the bag. "So explain that?"

I shook my head. "I dunno. You said there was blood in your room?"

Trystan nodded. "On the window."

"Inside or out?"

"Huh?"

"Was the handprint on the inside or the outside of the window?"

Trystan closed his eyes. I watched him, his eyes moving under his eyelids. "It was on the outside." He opened his eyes. "You said handprint. How did you know it was a handprint?"

I walked back to the couch. Several old volumes, all of them from the cache of books hidden in the secret compartment, were scattered on the cushion next to where I had been sitting. I found the black leather tome and showed the face of it to Trystan. A bloody handprint above silver engraving:

порекло

"It's called *The Ancestry* or *The Old Blood*. This doctor guy wrote it. It's a history of vampire hunters." Trystan looked up at me with a smile on his face. We were big fans of *Buffy the Vampire Slayer* when we were younger and I recognized that glimmer in his eyes. "Not the kind of vampire hunters you're thinking of. These are bad vampires, hunting what he called the Old Bloods, vampires like my mother and her family. The title's a play on words because the bad vampires really considered *themselves* the Old Bloods because they kept to the old ways instead of ..."

"What does this have to do with me and the bloody handprint?" Trystan picked up the other books and set them on the coffee table and sat down, folding his legs under him.

"It's how they mark you?"

"Mark me? Mark me for what? I thought I was already marked by you." Trystan's eyes followed me as I sat down next to him.

"They've marked you as a Blood Slave." Trystan was about to explode but I rushed on. "It sounds worse than it is. I mean if you hadn't already been marked, then yeah, it would pretty much suck. But my marking you protected you from the worst part of it."

"The worst part of it? It gets worse?" He wasn't sitting any more but paced along the bookshelves.

"Well, you know Renfield, from all the Dracula movies; does Dracula's every bidding, yada yada yada. I guess you could call him a Blood Slave. He has no choice; he has to do what he's bid to do. No free will." I watched Trystan pace. Mostly because he didn't seem like he was listening to m, I said, "Go make me a sandwich."

He stopped and looked at me. "What?"

"I said, go make me a sandwich." I grinned.

"Fuck you. Make your own damn sandwich."

"See. Not a Blood Slave. A giant douche, maybe, but not a Blood Slave."

Trystan scowled at me. "Why would they mark me as a blood slave. I mean especially when I'm not. I'm protected." Trystan stopped in front of the hidden bookshelf and ran a hand across the old books still lining the shelf. "There's so much we don't know." Melancholy filled his voice. "So what's the worst part?"

"They're targeting you." Trystan flinched at the words, as if struck. "To get at me, to get at my mother."

"I'm the weakest link."

I nodded. "I'm sorry Trys."

His grin, those eyes taking me all in, was a balm. "You can't keep apologizing for saving my life."

"I'm still responsible. If it wasn't for me…" He didn't let me finish.

"If it wasn't for you, what? I would have died in the forest? I wouldn't even have been there if it wasn't for you, so I wouldn't have died. This whole 'what might have been' thing goes nowhere.   You saved my life. Plain and simple. You apologize again, I'll have to kick your ass."   Trystan tried to keep a straight face.

Our laughter filled the library.

"God, I love you." The words silenced our laughter and he looked at me as he said it.

"Do you still?" I would have taken the words back if I could. I felt silly just saying them, but they were out before I even knew. I was dumbstruck at my own words.

"Well." Trystan stepped up to me. I noticed the flawlessness of his skin again, his scent intoxicating; and I could practically feel his pulse vibrating in the air between us. "I kinda have to. You're gonna be my hero."

I leaned forward and kissed him. He tried to pull away but I wrapped a hand around the back of his neck and pulled him to me.

"Jace. Stop. You'll. Hurt. Your. Self."   Each syllable came amidst torrid kissing.   Pain be damned. I kissed him again and again and again. His distress melted under my barrage and before I knew it we were pressed against the bookshelves. Books tumbled from the shelves and we stumbled over them. I wanted to keep kissing him but after one final long kiss I pushed away from him, staggered back and sank to my knees. My mouth was afire and I tasted blood. I flashed back to our first kiss when he had drawn my blood. The pain was exquisite, almost orgasmic. My eyes blurred, my heart pounded.

Trystan sank to his knees in front of me, his lips bloody. "Don't ever do that again." His words were breathless, his eyes vacant. I wondered if he was carried back to that same moment; to our first kiss. His chest rose and fell and I heard his heart racing. It was as if we had raced back to it.

I reached out to him and wiped the blood from his lips. The pain of contact was dull in comparison, but I flinched all the same.

Trystan grabbed my wrist and looked at the blood. "You know, we still haven't figured out who the guy was.   You said it was a dream, but the bloody clothes…I wore them in the dream. And I killed the guy. It's his blood."

"You're harshin' my buzz, Trys." I said.

"I'm serious Jace. We need to find out what's going on with him. Who he is."

"We don't even know *if* he is." My frustration must have been obvious as Trys met my eyes. "I mean, we know it was a dream. The handprint, that's real. The bloody clothes are real. The same person could have put them in your room. The rest, the tree, the sex, the killing, that was all a dream."

Trystan didn't look convinced but he nodded. "Maybe."

CHAPTER FIFTEEN

A Quickening Pulse III

THE

Fairweather Sun Times

WEEKLY NEWS   ISSUE MMMMDCCCLIV

Serial Killer Strikes Again

By Jason Steele

Sun Times staff writer
Authorities, including those with the county sheriff's department, Fairweather police department, as well as state official have concluded the sudden rash of murders to be the product of a serial killer. Anonymous sources within the police department have describe the most recent crime scene as "grisly" and "the worst I've seen." The victim, a nineteen-year-old student attending Fairweather Community College was last seen alive by his roommate in their English Composition

The roommate, who wished to remain anonymous until family members were notified, claimed the victim had seemed fine, aside from a cold. There was no official search for the victim, whose body was found by hikers in a wooded area just south of... <cont. page 9

Hero Revealed

Authorities, including those with the county sheriff's department, Fairweather police department, as well as state official have concluded the sudden rash of murders to be the product of a serial killer. Anonymous sources within the police department have describe the most recent crime scene as "grisly" and "the worst I've seen." The victim, a nineteen-year-old student attending Fairweather Community College was last seen alive by his roommate in their English Composition class Thursday night. The roommate, who wished to remain anonymous until family members were notified, claimed the victim had seemed fine, aside from a cold.   There was no official search for the victim, whose body was found by hikers in a wooded area just south of...

Tristan

I reread the article blocking out my internal monologue, though monologue would be somewhat of a misnomer, as all I really heard was a continuous bleating of "Oh no. Oh no. Oh no."

My mother was in the kitchen putting the waffle maker to good use. She hummed to herself, but I didn't recognize the tune. I could hear the sizzle of more batter being poured on the griddle and the sausage patties frying on the stove. Breakfast *was* the best meal of the day. Of course I doubt you'd hear me say that sitting in front of an extra large pepperoni pizza fresh from the oven.

"Trystan." I looked up. My mother stood at the table holding a breakfast platter of waffles. I hadn't heard her.

"Huh?" I stared up at her.

"You've been out of it for the last couple of days mister." She put a hand on my forehead, checking for a temperature. "Maybe we need to take you to Dr. Forrest for a check-up."

I shook my head. "I'm fine. I'm fine. " I grabbed three waffles and stacked them on my plate. I upended the bottle of Mrs. Butterworth's watching the gooey sugary maple goodness flow like lava into every waffle pocket.

My mother returned with the sausage and a cup of coffee for herself. "You say you're fine. But ..."

I took the plate of sausage from her. "You worry too much."

I watched her grin over her cup. "It's my job to worry too much. I'm gonna worry till the day I die. Get used to it."

She watched me eat. I've been told it's a spectacle. Her smile embodied maternal contentment as I reached for another waffle. Apparently at this table, gluttony was not a deadly sin.

Mrs. Butterworth made an unlady-like noise as I squirted out the last of the syrup.

"How's Jace?"

"Good." She waited for more and I couldn't help but think how we're always told to not talk with our mouths full and yet... I chewed faster. "He's good. Said thanks for the spaghetti. It was good." I crammed a whole sausage patty in my mouth. My mother frowned as I added some waffle to the mix. "How wa boo clubf?"

"What? Were you raised in a barn? Don't talk with your mouth full."

I laughed. I couldn't help myself.

"And book club was fine. I'd tell you about it, but your eyes are already glazing over."

#

"Did you see the paper?" I shoved the **Fairweather Sun Times** at Jace as he walked into the dining room. "I nearly shit myself when I saw it. What if...what if *that* was me?"

Jace scoffed but read the article, his lips moving as he read. He paled as he continued reading and slowly sat down.

"It was me." I rubbed a hand across my face and paced around the table.

I stopped behind Jace and read over his shoulder even though I'd already read the article several times. Jace tilted his head back. "Shhhh, you're mumbling in my ear."

I went back to pacing. "What are we gonna do?"

"Right now? Nothing. You just need to sit down. Let's just think about this logically."

I nodded and pulled a chair up next to Jace. He watched me wryly. "First, I didn't smell his blood or..."

"But you said I smelled different. That was like the first thing you said yesterday when I got to yours." I folded my hands together nervously, and then shoved them into the pocket of my hoodie. "Oh God."

"Would you calm the fuck down, you're making *me* nervous." His voice was harsh and he looked at me, surprised. "Sorry." He set the paper on the table. "This could all be just a coincidence."

"No such thing as coi..."

"Don't start with that crap."

"What? You can't tell me that it's a coincidence that I dream about killing someone out in the woods and the next thing you know we're reading a story about someone who's murdered in the woods."

"You forget, it said rash of murders. You only dreamed of one and they're saying that it looks like it's the same person: a serial killer. Unless you've been killing people and..."

That's true." I leaned back in my chair, relieved. The irony that I was relieved that there was a serial killer on the loose in Fairweather made me smile.

Jace grinned back in response. "You're welcome."

I'd kiss you right now if it didn't make you squeal in pain." I got up to clear my plate from the table.

"Kiss me anyway." He pulled me down by the sleeve of my hoodie and planted a kiss on my lips. Instead of squealing he pulled back and said. "I love syrup flavored Trystan."

"You better." I let him kiss me again; feeling a twinge of guilt at his pain.

Jace

Mr. Garrow glanced up from his desk as I walked in. "I need to talk to you."

"Does this have something to do with Mr. Cole? And him being marked." Mr. Garrow's grim disapproval caused me to step back.

"Maybe." I offered hesitantly.

He rose from his desk and pulled the door closed, shutting out the cacophonous noise from the hallway. He returned to his desk, sat down, straightened several pens and pencils on his desk blotter then looked at me. "How's Mr. Cole involved?"

I told him everything. The blood slave marking on the window, Trystan's dream, the bloody clothes, his scent and my reaction to it and finally the newspaper article. Mr. Garrow listened, fingers tented in front of him. "So I'm wondering is it possible? That he killed somebody? Shouldn't I be able to tell?"

"To answer your second question, yes, you should be able to tell. However, having never been in this situation before, who's to say what your reaction to him wasn't *the tell?* Right now, I'm hesitant to believe it. You made a valid point. This is the latest in a string of deaths. *If* Mr. Cole was involved, I think you would have had this reaction sooner due to the prior deaths."
Mr. Garrow looked out the window. He inhaled deeply started to say something then checked himself. I could almost hear the inner dialogue he was having as to whether to continue or not. He nodded to himself absently then looked at me knowingly.
"It is not unreasonable to believe that the *Old Blood* is involved. It's too convenient to call coincidence."

I've mastered the art of oblivious. "The *Old Blood?*"

"I'll need to talk to your mother. And father, of course." With that, Mr. Garrow rose from his desk and ushered me to the door. Apparently I was dismissed.

I found Trystan in the cafeteria. "So? What'd he say?" Trystan crammed the remaining half of a hotdog into his mouth. I'd never known anyone who delighted in food so much.

"Well for one thing, the first thing he asked was did it have anything to do with you."

Trystan stared fish-eyed, his mouth hung open, mid chew. It wasn't pretty. I reached over and lifted his chin, closing his mouth. He resumed chewing and I shook the sudden numbness out of my fingers. "Why'd he ask about me?"

"Well he did mention being marked."

Trystan scowled. "Have I thanked you for that yet?" He rubbed absently at the mark.

"But on the bright side, he doesn't think you're the killer. And then he mentioned the Old Blood. I played dumb."

"Yeah, you're a veritable LOLCAT."

"If that's your way of saying I don't have to play. Those are comic genius."

"I rest my case." Trystan dabbed a bundle of fries in ketchup. "How come you're not eating?"

I shook my head absently. "Pills. They're a great appetite suppressant. How many fat vampires do you know?"

"What are you saying?" I watched Trystan pat his virtually non-existent belly. "You callin' me fat?"

I couldn't help but smile. "Yeah you're my fat little blood slave." I had a feeling; if we were alone he'd be licking me like crazy until I took it back. The look he gave me told me as much as he shoved the last of his fries.

CHAPTER SIXTEEN

Blood and Tears

Trystan

The final bell filled the halls with a deluge, rushing for freedom. I had a finger curled in the belt loop of Jace's jeans, trailing behind him, watching his ass as he headed for our lockers. I yanked on his belt loop till his pace slowed.

"What do you think? A movie? You know, officially you haven't taken me out on a date yet. Some boyfriend you are." I smiled and bit playfully at Jace's shoulder.

"Oh, is that how it's going to be? Fine." Jace dragged me around the corner and pushed me into the art room and against the wall, his hands firmly planted on my chest. I could smell paint, oils and acrylics permeated the air. He gripped me by the hoodie and pulled me so close to kiss me but then stopped a hair's breadth away. "Trystan Cole will you *please*, please accompany me to a movie." His breath tickled my lips and the urge, *the need* to kiss him was so great, I had to press my head back against the wall for support. I could feel the nubs of push pins pressing against my skull and back. His eyes were intense, hungry. I licked my lips.

"Yes." Said the frog. I cleared my throat and tried again. Yes. What do you want to watch?"

His eyes were intent upon my lips as I spoke. "You pick."

I smiled. "*Frozen.*"

"We've already seen that." He whined.

"Yeah I know, but not on a date." It was my turn to lean against him. I maneuvered him until he was pressed against the wall. "Please." I pressed a hand firmly on his crotch and listened as he exhaled against my neck. I grinned and started humming along with Demi Lovato in my head as she sang *Let It Go*.

"You're very persuasive, Mr. Cole. Though the irony of *that* song at this moment."

I couldn't help myself as I gave him several quick squeezes and watched him arch his neck back and stare at the ceiling. I leaned in close and whispered in his ear. "Is that a yes?"

Jace nodded vigorously. "Yes. Definitely a yes. I think if you asked me I'd kick a puppy right now."

I laughed at that. "No need for that."

The movie started at 5:00. We sat in the lobby on a wooden bench and people watched.

"That one?"

"Hmm, I dunno. He doesn't look like threesome material to me." Jace scanned the lobby. I saw his eyes settle on a jock I recognized from school. He was tall and finely sculpted, even in his movie theatre uniform. "That one."

I watched him as he swept up popcorn. He seemed aware that he was being watched, but he was attractive; he was probably watched all the time; made girls all giggly and probably a few guys too. His arms were nicely toned and his ass was spectacular in a pair of tan khakis. I nodded unconsciously and Jace bumped my shoulder. "Hey!"

I looked at Jace and grinned. "Huh?"

"I'm the only one you can look at like that."

"Jealous?" I asked, still smiling.

"Yes." Jace's eyes were so intense, so vulnerable I swooned.

Frozen was perfection the second time around. Better than the first. I pulled the sleeve down on my hoodie over my hand and Jace held my hand. The armrest lifted up and we leaned in against each other. We shared our drink, two straws stuck in the lid. Once our cheeks brushed together and he inhaled sharply. I looked at him and muttered a quick "Sorry."

At the car after the movie Jace looked at me. "You're gonna have to kiss me now."

"But…"

"Hey, those are the rules. First date. First kiss." He admonished.

"But…" I couldn't help but smile at that. Certainly not our first kiss, but the sincerity in his voice gave me pause.

"You're not holding out on me, are you?" He feigned frustration. "Jace needs a lil' somethin' somethin'."

"Oh. Is that so?" I pushed him against the side of the car. "A lil' somethin' somethin', huh?" I watched him nod. At that moment he was definitely the most adorable thing on the planet. "Hmm. I dunno. You did buy me popcorn."

He nodded again and puckered his lips, leaning his head forward, closing his eyes. I laughed again. "God you're adorable. A big ol' dork, but adorable as hell."

He peeked at me, opening one eye. "Shut up and kiss me, damn it." He closed his eye again and re-puckered his lips.

I grinned. I honestly didn't think he was serious. It's not that I didn't want to kiss him. I just didn't want to hurt him. I let out a little squeak when he pulled me by the hoodie and kissed me.
Our foreheads bumped and then our lips. When the kiss broke he sighed and leaned back against the car.

My tummy growled.

"Okay, Cinderella…your chariot awaits. Let's get you home." Jace opened the door for me. I got in and watched him walk around to the passenger side.

I felt a chill as we pulled into the driveway next to my mother's car, the house completely dark.

Jace

It's the blood that I detected first. It's always the blood. The scent of it wafts through the air, a plume of life and vitality, but reeking of death. It is so rich; the air practically humid and heavy with it, I could almost taste it. I fought the bloodlust more than I have ever fought it before in my life.

A bloody handprint marked the front door. This one however had a cross marked on the palm.

I pushed open the front door and looked over at Trystan. His eyes expressed utter terror. No sounds came from the interior of the house but a living heat roiled out, like an exhalation, a death sigh we couldn't hear but felt on our faces. It was enough to get Trystan rushing past me and into his home.

"Mom!" Trys shouted out.

"Trys wait." I reached out to grab him, to hold him safe by my side but he rushed beyond my grasp and disappeared in the darkness. I listened as he called out again and again. The final time he cried out with a heartache and anguish that pierced my soul. I plunged into the dark house. The further I raced into the house, the stronger the scent. I came to an abrupt stop in the kitchen. Trystan sat crumpled on the floor, leaning back against the wall, his legs splayed. He held his mother's head in his lap. Her eyes stared blindly up at the ceiling. Blood; there was blood everywhere. He caressed her forehead, moving the stray hairs from her eyes.

The Blood of the Mark shall perish

The words were scrawled in crimson on the wall behind Trystan. His keening drew my eyes. I looked down at him, his eyes squeezed shut, streaks glistened his cheeks in the darkness of the kitchen. I slumped down next to him and pulled him to me, embraced him, his face buried in my chest: his tears soaking through my shirt and burning. His sobs shook us and I rocked him. I couldn't hold him tight enough. My anger raged inside as I stared up at the words.

This was my doing, no matter how inadvertent, had it not been for me...

Trystan gripped me tighter, his question muted in my chest. "Why?" It was a pleading laid at the feet of a 10 year old boy saving the life of his best friend.

"I'm so sorry." I kissed the top of his head, again and again, each kiss a jolt of pain, shocking me. I held onto him as he gripped me in a vice like grip; the pain indescribable; fiery. I imagined what a lash must feel like, across my back, across my chest, each slash digging into the flesh and tearing it away or a dull blade ripped across the skin. I held onto him tighter. It was no less than what I deserved.   I cried out in tortured agony, unable to take my eyes off the words. I don't know how long we stayed like that, in that hell of loss and pain, but I realized Trystan had fallen asleep.

"Trystan?"   His name came out in a whisper.   The overwhelming pain numbed me like a burning frost. I lifted him, staggering at the effort and carried him away from the carnage. His arms went around my neck, a wreath of fire. I staggered again, leaning momentarily on the doorframe before carrying on.

CHAPTER SEVENTEEN

Blood and Tears II

Jace

My father worried at the bottle cap, the pills rattling as he popped the lid off and on. The sedatives helped Trystan sleep but I was pretty sure my father would benefit a great deal if he took one or two himself. I'd never seen him like this, agitated and pacing; his anger as palpable and solid as the walls surrounding us. He lingered over my mother's shoulder and seemed torn. I wondered at that, for a moment, and realized the truth: he was going to have to tell her about the girl, my sister; their daughter; thought long dead.

My mother sat next to my bed, holding Trystan's hand as he slept. While the sedatives worked, he'd roused several times, yelling; had drawn fingernails down his cheek leaving raw angry scratches. Even as he slept the marks slowly healed, diminishing until there was no sign at all that he had hurt himself, except for the blood under his nails. He looked tranquil under the façade of sleep and I envied him that.

I found myself staring at nothing. My world and most assuredly Trystan's had just changed dramatically. I couldn't even begin to imagine his pain and heartache. As much misery as I felt, it was but a fraction of his own absolute desolation. I glanced over at him. He stirred fitfully, suddenly grimacing. I tried to will him peace of mind, but he gripped my mother's hand and minor tremors shook his body. She watched me, taking in my reaction: I rocked back and forth with nervous energy, and I know she wanted to come to me, to comfort me.

It's what mothers did. It's what Trystan's mother would have done were she here and the situation reversed.   I swallowed hard. I could feel tears welling and wiped at my eyes. I knew if I started I wouldn't be able to stop.

I needed something to occupy my mind, something to alleviate my guilt. I tried to mute the internal dialogue but there was no way around it. Had I not marked him in the first place would any of this have happened?   The answer was a resounding no.   I blamed myself and while Trys and I had had similar conversations concerning my actions and their repercussions, I felt certain when he woke, the blame would surely finally land squarely on my shoulders.

"Jace." I glanced up, startled, the room coming back into focus. My father and mother stood before me. He held her hand as she leaned down and kissed my forehead.   Her eyes glistened as she pulled back and I choked back a sob. She ran her hand down the side of my face, her thumb rubbing at what I assumed was a smudge of lipstick on my forehead.   My father cleared his throat. "Your mother and I…"

I nodded, looking out the window, the black of night visible only in halos of the amber streetlights and a radiant bulbous moon.   My father gripped my shoulder momentarily, a gesture of support that brought fresh tears.   I heard the door close quietly behind me as I rose unsteadily to my feet.   From the foot of the bed I crawled up next to Trystan.   He didn't stir, didn't move as I curled up next to him.   I rested my head on his chest, listened to the strong beat of his heart, almost felt it beating. The scent of his mother's blood was overpowering this close but I inhaled deeply. I would not forget this scent. I would not.

Trystan stirred beneath me and I held my breath.   He muttered; whispering, talking to himself, and telling himself not to look, that it wasn't real.   He became more agitated, more frantic and his hand shot out and grabbed my arm. I convulsed at the direct contact, my body bowing as if an invisible rope pulled me at my center mass towards the ceiling. I bit my tongue and tasted blood. I gulped in air. My heart pounded painfully. I tried to scramble away, try to pull my arm from his grasp, but his nails dug into my flesh and I watched curiously as blood began to pool around his fingers. The pain was exquisite.

Sublime beyond anything I'd ever felt, especially where his nails had pierced the skin. I couldn't breathe, I couldn't see, I didn't exist but within the hand's span of his grip. Somewhere far off, I heard a wailing so terrible, so sorrowful: it took a moment to realize it was me.

I continued to scream even after my father jerked me free of Trystan's grasp. He flung me to the floor and my mother and father both held me down. I was jolted back into my body, my breathing ragged, my vision blurred: completely disoriented.

My father held my arm, examining the angry wounds where Trystan nails had broken the flesh. I watched mystified as first he sucked on the would as if it were a snake bite and then he bit his wrist and a wash of my father's blood flushed the wounds. The fiery pain coursing through my body was extinguished almost instantly and my whole body collapsed. My father shook me, keeping me alert. I whimpered, too exhausted to speak coherently. He brushed back my bangs, which were drench and plastered to my forehead and peered into my eyes, raising the eyelids one at a time. My mother sat next to me on her knees, her lips were moving but I heard nothing but a hushed shhhhhhhhh; the snowy static of a television or the ocean.

I remembered when we were little we had gone to the coast on vacation. Trystan and I ran along the beach, splashed water, kicking it, squealing gleefully at the numbing chill and we pressed seashells to our ears. "It's the ocean." Trystan had said. I listened and listened and all I heard was that same shhhhhhhhh.

Afterwards, after the vacation when he would shush me, I would put a hand to my ear, like I held a seashell and he would scowl because he knew what I was about to say.

"I hear the ocean." I tried to tell my mother. My eyes were wet and I tried to blink away the tears as my mother lifted me up into a hug. She rocked me, my arms hanging limp. I felt nothing, my body numb and heard nothing but the shhhhh of the ocean.

CHAPTER EIGHTEEN

Blood and Tears III

Trystan

"Do you want some more pancakes, dear?" My mother's voice echoed from the kitchen.   It sounded like she was at the other end of the house and not on the other side of the swinging door.

"Yeah."   I crammed another forkful of pancake in my mouth. The taste was off, a little bitter. I poured a little more syrup on the stack; the syrup's hue not quite brown but closer to crimson. "How was your garage sale adventure this morning?"

The little syrup pitcher was a thing of antiquity that my mother had picked up at a garage sale. The platter she served her pancakes on also came from a garage sale; the neighbor across the street. She loved to find little knick-knacks especially for the kitchen. She brewed coffee from an old fashioned percolator: it didn't even plug in; you had to put it on the stove.   If she could get her hands on a wood-burning stove, I think she'd be in hog heaven.

I think that was her weekend mission. Every weekend, at the crack of dawn, she was up and out of the house, her little coin purse in hand, stuffed with one dollar bills, "easier to haggle with, if you don't have big bills" she'd say. And lots of quarters. The things she could get for a quarter would surprise you. She came home with lots of books, doilies, and she had a thing for Christmas ornaments. She had boxes and boxes of them. I worried the tree would collapse under the weight of them, but every weekend, rain or shine, she'd come home with another haul of ornaments.

"Guess what I found this morning?" I turned back towards the kitchen, waiting for her to come through the door with box of Christmas ornaments.

"I dunno?"

"You have to guess." Her voice was giddy

"Mom." I complained. "We play this game every weekend. I say 'Christmas ornaments' and you say 'no' even though you did and I call 'bullshit' and you yell, 'Trystan', all scandalized that I would dare say bullshit even though I say it every Saturday morning and then I say 'sorry' and that's when you come out of the kitchen with a box of...you guessed it, Christmas ornaments!" I cram a whole slice of crunchy bacon into my mouth.

The kitchen door swings open and my mother is standing in the doorway, drenched in blood, her throat a gory mess, her eyes dead and staring, her lips stretched into a rictus smile. In her arms a naked infant boy wriggles, arms and legs flailing, a smile on its face as it feeds on the blood dripping from my mother's ravaged throat.

"I found you."

I jerked awake, my heart pounding. I pulled myself up and glanced around Jace's bedroom. The curtains were drawn closed but ambient white light from outside lit the ceiling above them. I could just hear whispers coming beyond the bedroom door, but could make nothing of the words spoken. I closed my eyes, leaning back against the headboard. Visions of blood and gore, of my mother staring dead eyed at the ceiling flashed behind my eyes. I choked back a sob, biting the palm of my hand to keep from yelling out. I bit so hard I drew blood.

I don't know how much time passed; how long I stayed like that, I just knew that the light was different, softer, paler when Jace peeked in. I blinked away tears as he walked slowly towards me. He sat next to me, leaned in and wrapped me in his arms. There was no hesitation as I latched on to him, wrapping my arms around his waist and burying my face in his chest. I cried. My sobs drowned out his soft comforting words, though he whispered them close to my ear. All I could do was pull him tighter to me, gripping handfuls of his shirt; I could not get close enough. He kissed the top of my head, caressing my hair and I could only imagine the pain-filled grimace on his face as he tried to comfort me.

Again, I lost track of time.   No auriferous light outlined the curtains; no pale reflections bleached the ceiling.

Jace slept. This close, I could see his eyes moving under his eyelids, his breathing was quick and shallow and his grip around me tight. His arms trembled; his whole body shook. I wondered what pain he endured, while he slept with me in his arms.

I tried to disentangle myself, lifting his arm carefully. A spasm racked him, like a jolt of electricity shot through his body. I dropped his arm quickly only to notice small black crescents marred the inside of his arm.   I leaned in closer. I could tell they were fingernail impressions cut into his flesh.

"Hey." Jace's voice was coarse and weak. He pulled his arm back and sat up straight, shifting so he could lean back against the headboard.

"What happened to your arm?"

He shook his head, looking at the marks absently. "Nothing. It's fine."

I looked at it again, started to reach out and turn his arm so I could see it better but pulled my hand back. "It doesn't look fine. What happened?"

"You were dreaming. You reached out and grabbed me. It wasn't your fault, so stop looking at me like that." He touched the wound warily. "It's nothing."   His jaws were clenched tight as he spoke.

"You're lying."

"Trys. The last thing I fuckin' care about is a little scratch on my arm. I mean your mom…" He swallowed the last of it, his eyes shining.

I was still numb, drained of emotion.

"I'm so sorry. I… I… wish I could take it back. I wish…"

I stared at him blankly. I couldn't even form an emotional response.   There was no response. He couldn't take it back. There was nothing he could do.

My mother was dead.

I found you.

An image of the little boy feeding off of her blood sent shivers through me.

CHAPTER NINETEEN

A Touch of Fire

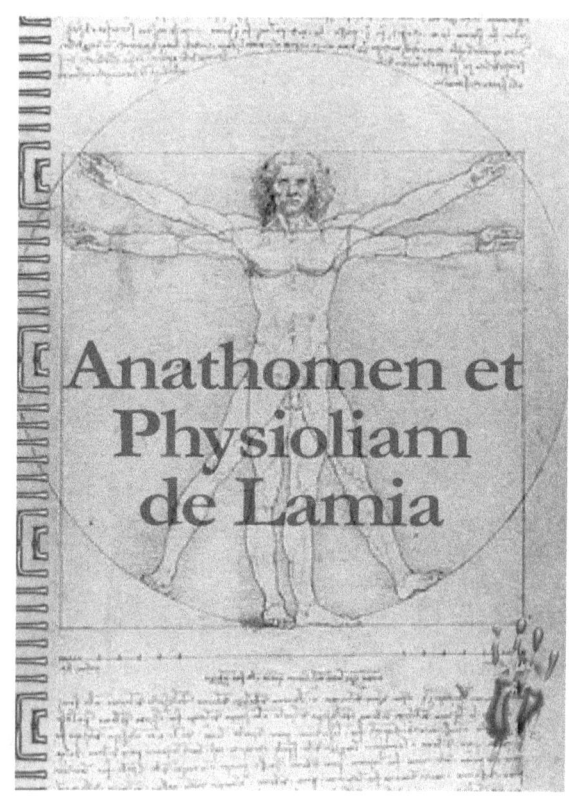

Jace

I woke with a start, my heart pounding, my arm burning, heat radiating from the spot where Trys had grabbed me, where his nails had pierced the skin. The wounds had healed completely in the night, as I slept, but still I felt his ghostly grip on my arm. I scanned the room, not mine, but my parents, looking for Trystan. I could feel him close by, a sensation I had not previously experienced. It took but a moment to know he lay asleep in my bed, I knew he dreamed, though not of what.

My own dreams were bizarre, dreams I'd had before, of death and dying, dreams of my own death.

It was eye opening.

I know I said that once you die, you're dead, but I have to amend what I said. Certainly, death is final and vampires can die, but as I said before, a born vampire's body is different. The physiology of death is a process much akin to aging; we are born and the aging process takes hold, understandably at a much slower pace. And death too, if it is not of the most extreme nature, the process of it, the shutting down of the heart and lungs, the brain and oxygen delivery, the process takes too long for a vampire to die of ordinary means. The regenerative capabilities of our bodies are far too efficient.

We are most vulnerable when we are younger. We are still stronger and more capable than the average teenager but up through adolescence a vampire is pretty much at the mercy of the environment, just like any other kid. Our immune system is immeasurably enhanced, so none of those embarrassing pimples, cold sores, pink eye, mono, warts, or sexually transmitted diseases. You want to discover a vampire in your school. Look for someone of natural flawless skin, perfect teeth, 20/20 vision and is physically fit. All modesty aside, vampires are visions of perfection.

But there is, what's called the phoenix code. A little sequence, unique to a born vampire's DNA, which brings about an extraordinary, some might go so far as to say; catastrophic change. The vampire body is tempered, much like a blacksmith will temper steel in fire. This tempering brings about an excruciating burning "death."   But much like a phoenix reborn from its ashes, so too does the teenage vampire rise from his apparent death.   Gives a whole new meaning to puberty is a bitch.

My dad tried to prepare me for it, but because my mother made him and he wasn't born, he didn't experience it first hand, so his preparation fell short of the mark.   Not that I blamed him, of course; how could I?   It wasn't like he could go to the library and pick up a copy of, *What's Happening to My Body for Vampires.*

"Are you feeling alright?"   My dad looked at me, a hint of concern in his eyes.   "You look a little pale."

The pale joke was part of his cliché vampire repertoire, his bedside manner, if you will.   He thought himself something of a funny man, though for the life of me, I didn't know why.   When it came to comic timing, my father was pretty stiff.   And even if the joke was even remotely funny, his delivery was lacking.   I think the only joke that he got right:

"What's the one question you never ask a vampire?"

And I'd go along with the joke.   "I dunno, what?"

"How's your stake?"   Only then he'd have to follow it up with, "Get it?   How's your steak... only it's stake;"   And he'd spell it.   "S T A K E, not steak; S T *E* A K cuz vampires don't like..."   And my rolling of the eyes or Trystan's muted laughter, not at the joke but at my reaction to the joke, is enough to send my father back from whence he came.   It was a source of great embarrassment.

I mentally prepared myself for the stake joke but my father sat down on the edge of my bed.   He held one of the books from the hidden library in his hands, the leather binding a deep burgundy.

"I found something."

I tried to sit up, pulling myself up on my elbows and then struggled up until I was leaning back against the headboard.   He'd held his place in the book with a finger and opened it easily.   The font was bold and dark, contrasting starkly against the pale yellowing pages.

"It's not really an answer.   But it's a starting place."

I reached over and lifted the book, looked at the spine of it, trying to discern the title of the book: *Anathomen et Physiologiam de Lamia* It was a formidable tome, inches thick, and the paper so thin it was practically transparent.. An image of Da Vinci's *Vitruvian Man* was embossed on the cover. Very little of the embossed gilding remained except for the outstretched arm closest to the spine of the book. I'd seen the book, had even gone so far as to pick it up and page through it, but it was written in Latin. I'd studied Spanish a couple of semesters, but the very notion of using my Spanish and its Latin base, as a source of understanding or interpretation was ludicrous.

"Okay. It doesn't look like it was a good something."

"It's the *tactum ignis.*" He ran a finger across the page as he reread. "It's called the touch of fire."

I nodded. That sounded right on the mark. "What causes it?"

He shook his head, reading quietly under his breath. "*et notam praesidio sanitatis....*the brand....no... mark of protection and health....healing....*ignus accensus...*burning fire...phoenix."

"Phoenix? Like the phoenix code?" I was shaking my head. The memory of it caused me to flinch.

My father reached over and took my wrist to calm me. "I don't know. Let's not jump to conclusions. His brow furrowed as he continued reading. "*et disperdam te, nisi in te amplecti, ad tactum ignis ardentis phoenix.*"

I cringed at the mention of phoenix again.

"What?"

"Well..."

"Just tell me."

"It's something along the lines..." He squeezed my wrist again for reassurance. "My Latin isn't strong and I don't know if the translation is correct. But it's something along the lines: the burning touch will destroy you unless you embrace the phoenix." He shook his head. "Except this is the word for sun and..." He shook his head.

My frustration was getting the better of me. "Dad?"

"I really should speak with Garrow. His Latin is stronger."

"But the Phoenix stuff. Does it have to do with *the phoenixstuff?*"

It sounded like I was talking in riddles, and I suppose if anyone else was listening, they might have thought so, but my father knew and he nodded.

It was the pain that I most feared. It was unbearable. I blinked away tears and swallowed my anxiety. I took a calming breath and tried to center myself.

"It's rare. What's happening to you with Trystan."

"Why?"

"Well, like most things, there is cause and effect. The initial trigger was the mark."

"But..."

"You marked Trystan when you were 10. You essentially gave him a booster shot at a moment when his whole system was in overdrive helping him to heal. Once his body healed, the mark went dormant. The few times he's hurt himself since then was no where near as calamitous and so the mark wasn't triggered again."

"It was *her*, wasn't it? "

My father nodded again. "Her attempt at marking him or turning him was an attack on his system that triggered your mark. You may have noticed his lethargy. His system went into overdrive again but this time he was perfectly healthy but the mark was fighting what she did. The problem, because you are brother and sister, your genetic makeup is so similar, the mark doesn't recognize the difference. The mark, it works on a molecular level and it activates the phoenix-coded sequence of your DNA – mRNA transcription. It literally burns. When he touches you, the mark is triggered and the physiological response is instantaneous.

I stared at him. It all seemed incomprehensible. I couldn't help but feel lost.

"I'm afraid, before too long, you'll not be able to be near him due to pheromonal interactions."

"I'm not going to be able to smell him?"

My father shook his head, the teacher in him taking over. "Contrary to popular belief, pheromones aren't scents, they have no smell but are chemical messengers that..."

"Dad!"

He nodded. "Yes, in essence, that's it. In layman's terms, you're allergic to him while his body continues to fight her bite. Physiologically, his body is doing everything it can to repulse you. The problem is that he needs your blood to fight her bite. Without it,..." My father stood and walked to the window. He drew the curtains wide and a shaft of dawning light lit the room. He stood straighter, nodding to himself, as if coming to a decision. "There is a solution."

I looked up, hopeful. But before he said it, I said. "I have to turn him."

My father said nothing, and from the other room I felt Trystan stir.

CHAPTER TWENTY

A Touch of Fire II

Jace

Trystan stood in front of the door length mirror in a pair of my boxers. He was trying to fix his hair, which stuck up every which way and made him, possibly, the most adorable thing on the planet. The boxers were distractingly enticing; hugging the curve of his butt cheeks.

The grin on my face was involuntary and probably a bit lascivious. I think I was actually drooling.

"What?" He looked at me in the mirror.

"Nothing. I was distracted." I sat on my bed and watched him pull on a pair of my jeans and my Dr Fluke and Smash 5sos t-shirt, which I'd had made online at one of those make your own t-shirt websites.

Trystan rolled his eyes. "Anyway."

"What? I'm not allowed to get distracted?"

"A stiff breeze distracts you."

"As long as it's stiff."

Trystan went back to his hair, his frustration evident. He grabbed a brush and tried overpowering it, but to no avail. He still looked adorable, whether he thought so or not.

"Want to borrow a hat?"

His eyes got real big. "Do I need one?"

I laughed. "Oh my god. You look perfectly fine."

Trystan smiled. It was a tight smile and I knew he was thinking of his mother. Everything reminded him of her.

Five days had passed since his mother's death. The police had come by three times. Their initial visit was a two-hour ordeal filled with relentless questions and subtle hints and accusations that left me furious. My fury was not so subtle as my father ordered me from the kitchen until the interview was over. I paced in my room, a caged animal, until Trys knocked on my door. I wrapped him in my blanket and then held him quietly, rocking back and forth, unable to talk, but shhhhh-shing him tenderly as he cried.

Their second visit was less accusatory and more of an update concerning their investigation. Her murder had been officially linked to a pair of grisly murders in the woods.

The third visit left all of us unnerved.

"Our families have known each other since the boys were born." My father stood at the window. It had started raining and the sky was dark with heavy rain clouds. He strolled back and sat in one of the easy chairs. The detectives were perched forward on the couch, glasses of ice tea in front of them on the coffee table. One had a notepad open and he wrote with a black pen, scribbling quickly and I could see the ink was almost gone. The other sat back and watched us, his eyes moving from one face to another and then back again.

"And you don't know of anyone who would do this."

My father shook his head and looked at Trystan and I. We both followed his cue and shook our heads.

"No one who had a grudge or was angry at your mother?" This time the officer leaned forward and looked directly at Trystan.

"My mother...everyone loved my mother." His voice was hushed but this time instead of sadness, he was angry. "Why...why do you keep asking me that?"

"I understand you're upset son. We're just trying to get to the bottom of this. Trying to find out who did it and figuring out

possible reasons why can certainly lead us in the right direction.
" He leaned closer to Trystan putting a hand on his knee.
"Sometimes, a little time, a little distance from the incident can
bring a clarity; help you to remember something." The officer
watched for any reaction then leaned back and looked at his
partner and nodded.

"The problem is, we're having a little difficulty finding a link
between your mother's murder and the two murders in the
woods." The officer scribbling in his notepad flipped through it,
for affect and then continued. "It's obvious the killer or killers is
the same, at least considering in so far as the amount of blood
and the condition of the ..."

Notepad cleared his throat and shook his head and the other
officer continued. "...but there's no link between the victims."
The officer rose from the couch and ambled over to the window
where my father had been looking. The curtains were sheer but
the dark clouds and rain obscured the view even more beyond
the curtains. He pulled one of them aside and peered out.
"When I was growing up, I remember there was a wooded area
about a quarter mile from my house. My best friend and I, we
were drawn there. And our parents were always telling us to
stay out of there. It was private property. You see." He turned
back towards us. "But we just couldn't stay away." His smile
was crooked and superficial. "Are you familiar with the
woods?" He nodded back towards the window and the large
copse of trees beyond. "Two curious boys like yourselves, I bet
you've been out there."

"When we were little." Trystan ran his hand absently across
the scar. "We had a fort. We tried to build a tree house,
but..." Trystan looked at me, grinning at the memory.

The tree house had been his idea. It was to be at the top of
the tree from which he had fallen. He was feeling invincible
after such a crazy fall and what better way to prove he was
invulnerable than to climb to the top of that tree and, as he liked
to say, make the tree his bitch. The logistics however proved to
be our downfall. Plus, his mother threatened to ground him for
the rest of his life if he went anywhere near that tree again. I
never told him that his mother manipulated a promise from me
to put an end to his plan. In the end we built a fort and he had

carved his initials deep into the trunk of that tree for any and all to see.

"Oh yeah?" The officer scribbled in his notepad and looked at his partner. "A fort?"

"I don't even know if it's still there." I don't know why I said it but both officers grinned in response. I hoped I wasn't squirming, and my father frowned imperceptibly. I had forgotten that that was where my father had found me after the incident at the Frozen Toad, the incident where I attacked Trystan and then lost 6 hours of time.

"Do you know a Zachary…" the officer flipped back in his notepad. "Holt, a Zachary Holt?"

"Yeah. Well not really. He goes to our school."

Both officers nodded. "We spoke with your principal. He mentioned an altercation between you and Mr. Holt; a fight."

"He jumped me in the cafeteria. I don't even know why. We.."

"We?" Good cop asked.

"Yeah, me and Trystan were having lunch and he jumped me. But Mr. Garrow broke it up." I didn't know if it was a good idea to bring Garrow into the mix, but it was too late as notepad was scribbling again.

"Mr. Garrow?"

"He teaches biology."

More scribbling. "What happened after the fight?"

"Huh?"

"After the fight, did he threaten you? Did you see him after that?"

I shook my head and from the corner of my eye, I could see Trystan shaking his too. "No. That was the last time I saw him. I thought he got expelled or something."

Notepad nodded his understanding

"Was anybody else there?" Good cop leaned forward and took a long drink of his ice tea, sounding appreciative. He put the glass back on the table and looked contemplative, as if remembering something. "A girl, maybe?"

"I think Zachary came into the cafeteria with a girl, but I didn't see her." Which was true. I sensed her but she had run after Trystan while I fought with Zachary.

"What about you?" Notepad looked over at Trystan who shook his head.

"No. I..." He looked at me. "Jace told me to run."

Both officers looked puzzled. "He told you to run?"

"He doesn't like to fight. " I offered. "And Zach was acting crazy. I didn't want him to get hurt." I felt cornered.

"So you ran?" They both looked at Trystan.

He rubbed his scar and nodded.

Notepad flipped through his notes again. "Do either of you know an Eddie Trace?"

I looked at Trystan and then at my father then at the officers.

"He was the first victim in the woods. He worked at Groovy Movies, right next to The Frozen Toad. I'm told it's a popular hangout."

Neither of us responded.

"He was also a student at Fairweather High. You sure neither of you knew him. Maybe had classes with him?" The officer seemed to be losing interest in this line of questioning or maybe he was feigning disinterest. It was obvious he already knew the answers, probably already had our class schedules.

Notepad sat back and flipped through his notes again. Flipping from one page back and forth a couple of times. "This mystery girl. I have a note here...." He nodded at his partner then looked at Trystan. "The security guard in the parking lot mentioned you and a mysterious girl. Said you were acting a little weird, talking about a girl. Then he says that Zachary Holt was acting the same way a week later, walking around, acting dazed, mentioned a girl. Both times, the security guard didn't see a girl but said both you and Mr. Holt were insistent that there was a girl.

"Trystan sat up straighter and leaned forward. "There was this girl. In the parking lot, she came up and kissed me. I didn't even know her. First she was there. Then she was gone." He looked at me and smiled. "'Member I told you about it and you thought I was dreaming it." We both smiled. "Told you it was real."

"Was this the same girl from the cafeteria?"

Trystan shook his head. "I don't know. I haven't seen her since the kiss. I was starting to believe it was all a dream, like Jace said." Trystan rubbed at his neck absently

"Officers?" My father spoke. I'd forgotten he was here I was so mesmerized by Trystan's act. "What does this have to do with the murders?"

"Well, Mr. Blackwell. According to witnesses of the altercation between your son and Mr. Holt, it appears as though this mysterious girl followed Trystan while Jace was fighting.

Furthermore, they said that as soon as the fight was over that your son raced off in the same direction. One witness puts the three of them in a classroom together. Said they were fighting with the girl and then afterwards that the two of them, your son and Trystan were..."

"It wasn't the same girl." Trystan stood up abruptly, bumping the coffee table. Notepad leaned forward quickly and caught his glass before it was knocked off the table. "She was stalking me. She threatened to tell everyone at the school about me and Jace. I tried to talk some sense into her. But she wouldn't listen. Then she attacked Jace and he just pushed her. They didn't really fight." He sat back down. "Not really."

"And what is her name?"

Trystan shook his head. "I don't know."

"So...first you have a mysterious girl who kisses you in the parking lot at school. A girl you didn't know and haven't seen since. And then you have another, completely different girl, this one stalking you and threatening to out you to everyone at your school, and you don't know who she is either?" Notepad looked at his partner and shook his head. "You can understand why I'm finding this hard to believe."

Trystan started to reply but had nothing to add.

"What are you hiding?"

It was my father who stood this time. "I think, unless there is some connection..."

"Mr. Blackwell. As I said before, we're just trying to get to the bottom of this whole ordeal. Certainly we're not accusing your son or Trystan, but something here is not right. These two young men have come in contact with at least two of the murder victims, if not all three of them.   Records at the movie rental store indicate that they rented a movie the week Trace was murdered. So the connection, Mr. Blackwell, seems to be these two boys." Good cop drank the last of his ice tea.   "We just want to know why. And that why may very well be this mysterious girl, who ever she may be."

CHAPTER TWENTY-ONE

A Touch of Fire III

Trystan

We buried my mother on a Sunday morning.

A gallery of gawkers and a couple of news van were far up on the hill behind two police cars; while at the graveside, it was just Jace's family and myself and three ladies from my mother's book club. They wept and dabbed their tears with white handkerchiefs. They told me how wonderful my mother was and hugged me tight before pulling back and straightening my hair or rubbing tears off of my cheeks. The sun played in and out of the clouds and gilded everything with morning light.

All I remember of the actual burial was Jace; his crying, the tug of my hand from my coat pocket and the moment he took it into his own hand. I looked at him and saw the pain crashing through him.

"It burns."

Jace's breathing was labored and he gripped the tabletop, his hand trembling, his knuckles white. There wasn't anything else we could do. My need for his blood had grown to the point where I was showing signs of withdrawal; my head ached, my hands shook with a trembling palsy, I was anxious and nauseated.   And there was a growing pain that pulsed with every heartbeat. I thought I could endure it but the longer I waited, the stronger the necessity, surging like waves of an incoming tide.   It was Jace who decided to put an end to my misery.   I shook my head even as he sliced into the palm of his hand and held it out to me. I took his hand gingerly and after another moments hesitation drank the pooling blood from his palm. I noted his reaction to my touch, his arm jerked in my grip, the muscles grew taut and his eyes grew distant as he watched me feed. As his anguish increased, mine dissipated simultaneously. While I needed his blood, I didn't need much of it. However it did have to be fresh.

It had crossed our minds that we could draw some blood and have it ready for me to drink; had actually filled a mason's jar with Jace's blood and hid it in the refrigerator.

The first time I drank it was also the last. It was noxious and I vomited it up after a minute of excruciating pain, far worse than the withdrawals. Whatever property his blood contained that I needed wasn't present in the stored blood. His father explained it after we told him what had happened.   "While normal human blood can be stored safely for approximately 42 days without any loss of efficacy, Jace's blood degrades almost immediately. It's vitality or life force, if you will, dissipates, much like the nitric oxide in human blood which keeps blood vessels open." Jace's fresh blood surged through me like a cooling balm.

"Better?"

I nodded, sinking back and wiping the blood from my lips. Having hungered for Jace for as long as I have, not in this literal sense, but hungered all the same, the taste of him, on my tongue and lips seemed inexplicably right.   There was nothing exotic about it, except maybe what it was doing to me, what it was making me feel, how it was making me feel. I couldn't help running my tongue across my lips to taste him again.

Jace didn't look so good. His father had told us that things were going to get worse.

"Jace?"

He raised his eyebrows as a response when he looked at me.

"What was your dad telling you the other day?"

"What do you mean?"

"He said things were getting worse, but..."

"He was telling you how we could fix it. Once and for all."

Jace looked down at his hands, running his thumb across the mending cut on his palm.

"I don't understand. You sound like it's a bad thing."

"It is." He looked up at me, conflicted. "Being around you is getting harder and harder for me; something about pheromones. I can't even breathe sometimes. It's like standing in a fire and breathing the hot smoke. But if I turn you, it'll all go away."

"Turn me? Into a vampire?"

Jace nodded.

"Annnnnd? That's a bad thing?"

"It changes you; not just a little bit, but it's like a genetic reboot. Everything. My mark will be gone. Whatever it did to you will be gone."

If that's what made me love you, that'll be gone, too. I fought that thought, denied it could be true, but part of me believed, feared, that perhaps it was true.

"The blood cravings will be gone too. I mean, you won't need *my* blood anymore." Jace's smile didn't reach his eyes. "And we'll be able to..."

"Why are you worried?" And he *was* worried. I could see it in his eyes, hidden behind the smile and the blush that suddenly colored his cheeks.

"I don't know." He started to say something but stopped. He rubbed the back of his neck before starting again. "When mom turned dad, she said it changed him. Not in a bad way, but it changed him. There was something...I don't know... wistful about the way she said it, like she missed him, like there were two of him: the one before and the one after."

"And you think I'm gonna change?"

Jace nodded "I've been a part of you since we were ten, literally. We've been a part of each other all our lives, but when I turn you, that'll be gone."

I wanted nothing more at that moment than to kiss him. His fear was tangible. I could feel it or maybe it was my own fear.

"I don't want to lose you. And there's a chance…"

"Jace. I love you. And you're never going to lose me. You're stuck with me." I ran my fingers along the sleeve of his shirt, playing with the button at his cuff. "You're my family now."

"If you say I'm like a brother to you, I'm gonna bite you."

I fought the grin. "A brother from another mother?"

"I knew you liked it when I bit you."

I waggled my eyebrows. We both looked at the scar: his mark.

"It *was* kinda hot." It suddenly occurred to me that he hadn't bitten me since the revelation that he was a vampire. It also occurred to me that when he next bit me, he would be turning me. "Is it gonna hurt?"

"Yes."

I didn't want to ask if it was going to hurt a lot. "Okay."

Jace gazed at me and nodded, his eyes glassy with tears. "We don't have to. I mean, not right now."

"What do I have to lose?"

The look in his eyes put words to my own thoughts.

Everything.

CHAPTER TWENTY-TWO

Anathema

Trystan

"It's gonna hurt."

"Well duh! I figured that. So far everything about this has hurt. If it's not me then it's you. I can't even touch you!"

"You don't have to yell." Jace twisted his dirty napkin and threw it in the empty plate. We were in a sports bar, with six big-screen TVs behind the bar and unlimited appetizers on the menu. It was a knockoff of Hooters, but the boobs were wasted on us.

We had taken one of the tabletops and were perched on high barstools, sharing crunchy onion rings and cheese fries and chicken nachos; I had finally gotten my appetite back.

The noise in the bar was loud enough to cover our conversation. I leaned forward over the table towards him. "I'm sorry." I was feeling extra bitchy and I couldn't articulate properly so I was taking it out on him. He did this to me. It was his fault. But I couldn't say that. Not now. Not ever. Especially after what happened to my mother. Because that would mean her death was his fault too.

The waiter in the bar area ambled by and switched out our empty Dr. Peppers with new ones and took the empty onion ring platter. "Anything else?" He had pretty eyes. They were a dark chocolate brown, deep and soulful. I was pretty sure his eyes, as well as the perfectly contoured jeans he wore helped increase his tips.   Especially in a bar full of well endowed women.   The eye candy for the gay sports fan was limited.

We both shook our heads, then watched him walk back around the bar.   Jace smiled to himself and I felt a momentary sting of jealousy.

"What?"   He nudged my leg under the table.

"Huh?"

"You look mad."

I shook my head.   "It's nothing.   Just jealous I guess."

"Aww."   Jace smiled.

"Oh shut up.   It was bad enough when you were dating girls.   Now I have to worry about everybody."

"You don't have to worry about anybody."   He leaned in closer to me.   "I'm all yours."

"Well just so you know, I'm the jealous type."   I crammed a nacho covered in cheese and chicken into my mouth before I could say anything else.

His smile maddened me just a bit more.

"Oh, I know."   He looked back over at the bartender.   "You're kinda obvious.   I might have to warn the bartender to watch his back."

"Shut up.   I'm not that bad."

"You didn't see your face."   Jace started to say something else but stopped himself, then grabbed his Dr. Pepper instead.

I looked at him then looked over at the bartender who was wiping down the bar and staring at us.   He winked.   I gripped the table and glanced up at the big screen TVs instead.   Soccer players ran the length of the field on one screen while on the next screen there was a baseball player throwing a handful of sunflower seeds in his mouth.   The next screen had news scrolling across the bottom while a blonde pointed to a traffic map, emphasizing lines of red with arrows flowing slowly in one direction while green arrows flowed quickly in another direction on the traffic map.   After another moment I saw Notepad and his partner on the television.   My eyes must have looked huge.   I looked at Jace who was watching me.

"What?"

I gestured towards the bar.   "Third screen."   We couldn't hear what the policeman was saying but a scroll across the bottom of the screen told us there was breaking news in the case. A source close to the police believed another body had been found in connection to the recent string of murders. Jace looked at me and then at the TV.   When a photo of Mr. Garrow flashed across the screen and a brunette reporter started broadcasting live in front of the dark high school, Jace bounded from his stool, sending in crashing to the ground.   A few of the patrons stared as I pulled a couple of twenty dollar bills from my wallet and left them to cover our bill.

I don't know how, but Jace knew exactly where his parents were as he raced through the house and skidded to a halt at the French doors in the library leading to the patio. "What happened?"

Mr. and Mrs. Blackwell sat on the wrought iron furniture out on the deck.   Mr. Blackwell shook his head. Jace's mother leaned against her husband, burying her face in his shoulder, muting her sobs.   I looked at Jace and then back at his parents. "What's going on?"

"Mr. Garrow was my uncle; my mother's brother."

"I don't understand."

Jace went back into the library, to the hidden cache of books. I recognized the volume he pulled out.   It was the book that traced the bloodlines.   We had looked at it for Jace's family line but paid no attention to any of the other lines.   He paged through it quickly to the Garrow lineage. I noted the spelling had been changed, that it was originally Garou. I also noticed that the family was older than the Blackwell family by several hundred years.

"The Garrow are of the old blood.   When Lew..."

Mrs. Blackwell drew herself up straight, stood quickly and left the patio. The three of us watched her go. Jace's father continued after she disappeared beyond the library. "When Lewis married, he went against the wishes of the family. He was exiled, made anathema. Jace's mother hasn't seen nor spoken to him since." I looked back in the direction Jace's mother had left. I couldn't imagine her pain, her loss. It seemed ridiculous having just buried my mother.

I felt the weight of Jace's hand on my sleeve.

"I would have told you but..." His eyes followed mine. "I couldn't. She let Dad talk to him. There were things they needed to know, but I couldn't act any different. I wasn't supposed to know. If anyone found out..."

I nodded. Not that I understood the ramifications, but there was someone killing people, so I had a notion.

"You two should go on up to bed. In the morning we'll talk about what to say. Chances are the detectives will be here. I don't know if he had anything connecting us, but you already mentioned him to the police.

Jace ducked his head.

"It's alright." He clapped Jace on the shoulder and rubbed his back reassuringly. "No one knew this was going to happen. Now go on. Upstairs. We've more to worry about than the detectives.

I followed Jace up the stairs. We passed his mother in the living room; she spoke softly on the phone, murmuring unintelligibly until we were out of earshot.

In Jace's room, we sat on separate sides of the bed.

"What did he mean, we have more to worry about?"

"It's probably the Blood Council."

I watched him pull off his shirt and jeans. His boxers were bright yellow SpongeBob. I couldn't help but laugh even as I yearned to touch him. Instead I pulled on some of his PJs and climbed into bed.

I lay down, looking at the crisscross of shadows from the window. "What's the Blood Council?"

"Well, for one thing, they investigate vampire deaths. Most vampires don't die from natural causes. They have to keep the truth from getting out." Jace fluffed his pillow.

"And?"

"What?" Jace pulled the sheet up over me then draped an arm over me.

"You said for one thing?"

"Oh." Jace turned quiet.

I turned onto my other side where I was facing him.

"What?"

Jace took a deep breath. "The Blood Council decides if I can turn you."

CHAPTER TWENTY-THREE

Anathema II

Jace

"You're not serious."

Trystan is angry. Not that I blame him. I'm a little pissed too. I mean, after everything we've been through …

"Tell me, you're not serious." Trystan sat up and stretched across me to turn on the lamp. His scent was intoxicating and it hit me like a wave. The room rocked off kilter and I grabbed the mattress to steady myself. I fought the urge to kiss him and even more to bite him.   I closed my eyes and struggled with the yearning, fighting it and what frightened me most was that its will was becoming increasingly more powerful. I tried shallow breaths, but could taste him on the air.

I rolled away from him and sat up, and pulled my shirt up like a mask over my face.

His anger rolled off of him in waves. It was intoxicating. I shrugged off the sheet and went over to the window and slammed it up, gulping in the fresh air.

"What if they say no?"

"They won't."

"What if they do?" Trystan's voice tore at me.

"Trystan." I turned around feeling the cool morning breeze blowing against my back. Inches from me, Trystan stood; the heat of his body melted my resolve. I gripped the windowsill.

"They can't stop us. Even if they say no." I felt a stabbing pain in my gut and flinched, curling into the pain.

"You need your pills?"

I nodded. Trystan backed up slowly and a morning boner tented his boxers, but whatever anger he might have felt suddenly evaporated. In its place was love and concern and I had to avert my eyes. I heard the mint tin rattling as he grabbed it from the bathroom.

I took the moments away from him, to gather myself, my wits, and my determination, to fortify my resolve. I didn't know how much longer I could do this. It was getting harder and harder to fight. I was afraid.

"Here." Trystan held a glass of water and three of the red pills

He dropped them in the water and I watched the effervescent pills shade the water to a deep red. I could smell a coppery scent and like Pavlov's dogs, my mouth was awash with saliva. I took the glass in shaking hands. Some of the bubbling liquid sloshed onto my hands.

"Thank you." I drank it in several quick gulps. I could feel it acting, coursing through me, even as it filled my mouth. It was a calming balm, which my body absorbed quickly. "I need more." My throat was raw, my voice a hard rough growl.

Trystan nodded and started to turn away but I reached out to him and grabbed his arm. I pulled him to me and before I could even think what I was doing I bit into him, tearing into his throat hungrily. I could feel the flesh ripping and his body convulsed as I drank. His struggles were short lived, he pushed at me weakly and his tears wet my cheeks. I could taste their saltiness mixing with the blood and I drank all the more. I felt his pulse weakening and finally he hung limp in my arms, the spark of life in his eyes snuffed to a dull lusterless death. I dropped his corpse.

The thud woke me. My heart pounding, my breathing heavy, I looked over at Trystan. His eyes fluttered under his eyelids. His head lay awkwardly on his pillow and his throat was bared to me. I shuddered and leaned into him, inhaling deeply. I could do it. Right now. I could change him. Make him mine for all eternity. I could feel my fangs pushing through my gums: if you've ever felt the slice of a razor; it's almost silky as it slices through the flesh. I kissed his neck softly, the sting of it jarring.

I heard the thud again. My hearing was acute. I listened intently. I heard no footfalls, no breathing, and no push pull thump of a heartbeat.

There are myths about vampires, that we don't eat, that we don't actually breathe, that our hearts do not beat, but all of these are false truths.   The truth of the matter is that our bodies are so much more efficient that it may appear to be true.   Our hearts are larger and stronger and the thud of my heart is as efficient as ten hearts working in concert. While I could not hear my own heart beating, the sound of it, of a vampire's heart, is familiar to me, and I would recognize one, especially one that was foreign.

I went to the window first. It wasn't open and I checked the locks pushing them home. I scanned the surrounding yards, but saw only the flash of cat's eyes glowing under a bush at the far edge of the property.

Thud

I looked at Trystan. He slept peacefully. I longed to crawl in next to him and hold him, to kiss him, without the pain of a jagged blade ripped across my skin.

Thud

The vampire heart grows stronger with time, becomes more efficient. The beat is a drum echoing in a great hall; the strongest and oldest of hearts can be felt, reverberating through the air like a percussive wave to those keenly aware of it.

I stood at the door certain I felt the wave of an old heart. I'd never felt anything like it, anything so strong. Mr. Garrow had had a strong heart and I had felt it in class at times, in the quiet calm when the room was quiet. Many heartbeats but Garrow's was like a metronome beating the chords of time. I had asked my father how old Garrow was, but my father only shook his head, unable to answer.

Thud

This heart, I heard, I *felt* through the walls. It reminded me suddenly of Poe's *The Tell-Tale Heart*. I remember reading the story and thinking to myself that it was a vampire's heart that he heard and not the corpse under the planks. It was madness and guilt that drove him to confess, but the beating heart was that of a vampire's, pounding so greatly, what else could he think.

I opened the door and peered into the inky darkness of the hallway. No motion drew my eye. I stepped softly into the darkness and drew the door closed. I wished suddenly I could lock it against whatever I heard. But I knew no lock could keep him safe from this.

Thud

In the hall I could hear my mother and father in their sleep. Or I assumed they slept. If I heard this heart, most assuredly they heard it too, at least my mother who was of the blood. Their rhythmic beats were calm, while my own heart beat irrationally. I crept along in the darkness, my back against the wall.

Thud

I thought, but surely I was mistaken, but I thought I could actually hear the push of blood through the veins of this creature, this being. It was a soft sound, like silk drawn across a polished wooden floor, like a long drawn sigh. And then the pull of the heart, as the valve expanded, drawing the blood back.

I paused outside the door to the spare room.

Thud

I opened the door. The scent was subterranean, earthy and wet. The darkness in the room was unlike anything I'd ever seen or felt. It was oppressive, it was tactile; a humid thickness that flowed through the doorway. I could feel it against my bare feet. I stepped into the room, hesitantly. The air was frigid and were there light, I'm certain I would see my breath.

Thud

I shivered when I felt the presence; vitality so strong, so potent, the essence of life. The very darkness around me sprang into existence, swirling before my eyes and the yearning I felt for Trystan paled in comparison to the overwhelming hunger that hit me and knocked me back.

I heard a rumbling, low and filled with mirth. Laughter.

"You are a strong one. The blood flows strong in you."

The light nearly blinded me when he opened the curtains. The moonlight flared through the glass and illuminated him. He practically glowed, as if he out shone the moon. His features were classically handsome, sharp jaw, Roman nose, and his eyes pierced my very soul. There was something familial about his appearance.

He raised his head slightly, as if sensing the air around us. He angled his head and looked at the wall that separated this room from my own. I did the same and I knew he heard Trystan. He focused again on me. What light was in his eyes dimmed and I felt an emotional rift.

"I am sorry. You have a duty to your line, to your blood, to me."

The crash of glass jarred me and I shook my head. I felt as if I were awakening from a dream. I heard a muffled yell and I raced back through the hall, to my room.

The bed was empty, the broken glass shimmered in the moonlight. Trystan was gone.

CHAPTER TWENTY-FOUR

Anathema III

Trystan

The first thing I noticed was the blood. I didn't see it, but the coppery scent of it was such, that I could almost taste it in the back of my throat. I wondered if perhaps the blood was mine.

He, it, I don't know, but whatever it was, had crashed through the window in a flash of shattering glass that rained down on me. I had a moment's awareness before it was atop me, crushing the breath from my lungs, a grip so tight around my throat I cried out from the pain. And then everything was dark.

A pitch inky darkness surrounded me now and I lie on a floor of rough hewn stone. I reached up and tentatively ran fingers across my throat. The flesh was warm and tender to the touch, stinging and wet, like a burst blister. The wetness wasn't viscous, but slippery and I put my fingers to my lips to taste; it wasn't blood but salty sweet, the taste of tears.

A sibilant whisper and a rapid rhythmic ch-ch-ch-ch that I associated with insects, with black beetles, their carapace shiny and black, filled the darkness. I couldn't help but brush my hands quickly across my bare arms at the imaginary; at least I hoped they were imaginary, things crawling across my flesh. I shivered, my mind filled with chilling images.

It took me a moment to realize too that I wasn't alone in the darkness. I peered into the pitch black and felt or imagined eyes watching me.

"Who's there?" I listened. I thought there was a pause, a momentary break in the rhythmic sound. The darkness felt solid, pressing down on me or maybe it was the presence that I sensed. The darkness was cold, but I felt or imagined a plume of heat; a breath, perhaps, caress my cheek. "Hello?" I called out again.

"Do you know what you are?" The voice was ancient and filled my every sense. The sibilant whisper and the rhythmic ch-ch-ch-ch had gone silent, as if the very earth waited with bated breath. I shied away from the voice. It was too close. I pulled myself up, hugging my knees to my chest against the chilling darkness.

"What do you want?"

"It has nothing to do with want now, boy. It is need. It is *need* that forces my hand." There was disdain in that voice. And hatred.

"I don't know what I am. I don't know what you want....or *need.* I'm just me. Nothing special."

I felt his laughter before I heard it. It was deep and the air vibrated with it.

"What?"

"It cannot be so." Astonishment filled his voice. "Anathema."

"What does that mean?"

"The blood of the mark shall perish."

I saw the words. They had been scrawled in blood on the wall above my mother's savaged corpse. "You." I couldn't bring myself to say it.

"Killed her? No. Had I but known. Truly known." The wonderment lifted his voice.

"I don't understand." I rose to my feet, disoriented. I reached out to steady myself on something, anything, but there was nothing to grasp but darkness.

"Her death was in vain." The voice came from behind me and I turned quickly. The hand that gripped my arm was cold, but the grip was strong, vise-like, with nails that dug into my skin. I felt a burning and struggled to free myself, but his hold only tightened. When his nails actually broke the skin, the pain flared like fire surging through me like a current. I shook violently and my head slammed back against a solid chest. Another arm reached around me and held me up as my legs gave out. I struggled to breathe and the darkness suddenly flared to white.

Slowly, blurry images came into focus. I didn't know where I was.   The rough hewn stone under me felt familiar., but now I could see it, a marbled granite with glistening flecks.   Sconces held torches that lit the cavernous room in amber light. Large tapestries, depicting battles and pastoral scenes hung the length of the walls.   I drew a deep breath, the air warm. I reached up to feel my neck again, expecting another blistering sting, but the flesh was whole and cool to the touch. I could feel my pulse easily. I sat up, fighting a moment's disorientation: the room spun and I had to steady myself on the granite floor.

"It's true." The man stood tall in the arched doorway. I hadn't heard it open.

I just looked at him. He was old, but I recalled the strength he possessed when he held me firmly. It would be easy to mistake him for someone frail, but I had a notion it would be a deadly mistake to do so.

"What do you want?"

"As I said, it is beyond want, now." He strode gracefully until he stood a few paces from me. "Are you hungry? I can have something brought to you."

"No." My stomach growled in betrayal and the old man smiled. I tried not to snarl, but even more so, I thought how wonderful a couple of pieces of buttered toast would be.

"Are you certain?" The man stepped aside and I saw her.

"You." The girl, Jace's sister, stood holding a silver tray. Looking at her, I could see the similarities between her and Jace, but even more so the similarities with Jace's mother.   She smiled tentatively which gave me pause. It was so much like Jace's

I scrambled to my feet and took a step towards her. She edged back and the old man held a hand between us.

"I see you know her. You know who she is."

I nodded. "She's Jace's sister. They thought she died."

The tray of food dipped as she staggered back. She was puzzled. I looked at the old man again.

"You didn't tell her? Or... or... you lied to her. You told her..."

"It is customary in certain societies to discard female children and I told her this."

"You lied to her!" I was baffled at my own anger.

"Out of necessity. She is of the Blackwell line. The last female." The old man sighed as if he tutored a simpleton. "You are of the Cole line."

"I don't..."

"Perhaps it was ineptitude, but when families immigrated to this country and they were admitted into the country they're names were changed. Certainly not purposefully, but through a variety of reasons. The Cole family line is a long one. Almost as long as the Blackwell line." The old man stepped forward and took my hand. He lifted it and maneuvered my hand, palm up. With the nail of his forefinger he wrote out my last name, cutting the skin. I watched as the cuts healed slowly leaving a white scar of my name. "Before your name was Americanized to Cole, it was Kohl." He cut the name on my palm. The sensation of his nail slicing through the flesh was barely discernible, though I jerked my hand instinctually, but he held it firmly in his grasp. Again I watched the wound heal itself.

I still didn't understand what he was getting at. Jace's sister had put the tray down. On it, besides a plate of fruit and some toast, which caused my tummy to growl, was a book. A book that looked oddly familiar, a book much like the one from the secret cache in the Blackwell library. It was the book of lineages.

He released my hand and I rubbed it absently on my jeans.

He followed my glance at the book. "In ancient Egypt, when a child is born, it is marked."

My head shot up at that. *Marked.* My thumbed played along the scar on my arm.

"The Egyptians would mark the eyes of their child. Some said it was to strengthen the eyes, to enable them to see better. Some say, it was to protect the child from being cursed."

"What does any of that have to do with me?"

"Everything. The mark was made with kohl. Kohl is black, and the kohl was often carried in tubes or small jars. In some instances, those jars were called..."

A chill ran through me as I finished his sentence. "Blackwells."

CHAPTER TWENTY-FIVE

The Blood's Corruption

Jace

"We can't just sit here and do nothing!"

My mother smiled. It was an uneasy smile. She knew she was treading on very thin ice. "We know where he is. He's safe." She tried calming me, but I noted a lack of conviction in her voice.

I shook my head. "With the Blood Council?"

"Honey…"

I jerked away from her. "I don't care. I want him safe with me. Fuck the Blood Council."

"Jace, you'll not talk to your mother like that."

I glared at my father. He was angry too. How he kept calm seemed a bit miraculous to me. But he did it all the same.

My mother had known all along; had known everything, well almost everything. She hadn't known about her daughter, my sister. But everything else, the Cole family line, it's connection with the Blackwell lineage. At first I thought that made Trystan a vampire. But my father shook his head.

"It has to do with the fire. The burning." My father looked at me. "Do you know how they make charcoal?"

I rolled my eyes. The following hour was filled with his surprisingly animated history of coal, charcoal, colliers, (people who both made charcoal as well as people who mined coal) the word color and its origin from the Latin *colos* and *celare* which was defined as to hide or conceal. Which was apparently the perfect segue-way to makeup and how the ancient Amazonians used coal, the Egyptians used kohl, and even today coal tar was an ingredient in cosmetics. By the time he was finished, I had completely forgotten why he was talking.

"Even today, you'll find football players who put black under their eyes to protect them from the glare of the sun."

"Dad." I stared blankly, overwhelmed. "I just need to get to Trys."

My father nodded. "I understand. But he is safe. The Council will not harm him. Quite to the contrary, he's rather like the prodigal child."

I looked at him. "I don't understand. I mean he's not one of us. So how can he be a prodigal child?"

My father hefted one of the thicker tomes off the kitchen table. He had read from it before when he was trying to explain the touch of fire. Under it was another formidable volume, bound in sandy-hued leather with the title embossed in black.

رسمها فيوضحالنهار

My father pushed the book over. I don't know why, it's not like I could read what it said. Instead I just stared back up at my father, waiting.

He ran two fingers across the title. "My Arabic needs..." He shook his head. "It's titled, Drawn into Daylight. It's a history of sorts, a history of vampires, considered by many to be one of the earliest of vampire fictions. Because everybody knows vampires can't come out during the day." He deadpanned the last part, his voice painted with a hint of disdain. "The book tells how vampires came out of the dark and into the light. How a powerful sorcerer tried everything to save the love of his life. All of his attempts proved useless against the blood's corruption. There was no cure. He thought she was lost to him. But before the final transformation, the magi marked her, to protect her from the vampire who had turned her. It was inadvertent, the results: what he did because she was the first vampire to walk in daylight. She was the first to bare a vampire child. She was the proverbial Eve, the wellspring from which our kind has flowed. She bore two children, a girl and a boy. The girl was a vampire; the boy mortal. However the magi grew fearful. The mother and girl were still vampires, base creatures, corrupted. They hungered for blood and the infant boy was not safe. So the magi stole away in the night with the infant child to keep him safe. Where he carried him off to, no one knew, as he marked him to protect him from ever being found."

I started to ask the obvious question but my mother answered before I could put thought to word.

"She was the first Blackwell. And you are a direct descendant. Just as Trystan is. He is of the mortal line."

I wrinkled my nose. "We're related? Like cousins?"

"The term distant-cousins was never so fitting. The bloodlines are so far removed as to be meaningless. Thousands of years and countless generations."

"But the book on lineages dates the Blackwell line to like 700 years."

My father looked down at the book. "The Blood Council would have this book burned. Very few are still in existence. It is anathema."

"Why?" I ran fingers across the surface wishing I had my father's knack for languages. I wanted to read it.

"Because of the revelations." He looked at me. "What did my story tell you?"

It felt like I was in school. I rolled my eyes. "That my great great times infinity grandmother got it on with Harry Potter's great grandfather and poof here I am."

My father grinned wryly.

"And?"

"And that's why I can walk in the daylight?" I asked hesitantly.

"And?" He nodded, his eyes hopeful.

"Just tell me. I'm really not in the mood for a quiz right now." I slouched back into my chair.

"It told you that you *can* walk in the light. But the implication is rather more important. You *can* walk in the light, but there are those, the old blood, who cannot. The lineages is a necessary lie. For all intents and purpose, the old blood, the base night creatures of lore, are just that, myth and lore. The Council has meticulously cleansed history of their existence. They are the stuff of myth and legend."

I shook my head. It felt like I was missing something. Something big. "What does any of this have to do with me and Trys?"

My father looked at my mother. She stepped closer to him and wrapped an around his waist. "It is believed by some, who have read the histories, the true histories, that the child of a Blackwell Cole mix would end the corruption and purify the blood. It is this belief that has driven the Blood Council for a millennia."

"But we're guys. We can't...." The memory of my sister walking through the cafeteria her eyes intent on Trys silenced me.

CHAPTER TWENTY-SIX

The Blood's Corruption II

Trystan

"It is true, then?" I heard a sense of marvel in his voice. He looked very much like Jack Nicholson pre axe-wielding "here's Johnny" from *The Shining*. His voice sounded like Jack too, only more the general "you can't handle the truth" from A *Few Good Men;* either way, I felt a phantom menace that left me disconcerted.

He wasn't talking to me, though he regarded me as if I were some grand illusion, a trick of the light, like he'd been down this road before, numerous times, and maybe, finally, he'd arrived at his final destination. There was a craving in his eyes, a hunger, for what I didn't know, but whatever it was I had a feeling it wasn't good.

In response, my captor merely nodded, almost imperceptibly. It felt like a trial; judge and jury flanked the table on both sides. My first impressions were simple superficial ones. They were an ancient lot, by the look of them, and probably much older than I could fathom. They were all men, most of them showing more than a touch of gray at the temple, all dressed in an attire reserved for the wealthy and by the look of them; they were fully impressed with themselves and all that they represented. None of them spoke but deferred to the man on the monitor. Like him, they all looked at me like I was the second coming, a miracle made flesh. It was kind of creepy.

I think we were underground. I was escorted here from my well-appointed accommodations, (read: prison cell) to what appeared to be a conference room with a satellite uplink. There were a dozen of them in all, including three faces, one large and two smaller ones, staring out from a large digital screen on the wall. No windows, no views, no soft light filtered through curtains, the walls were blank save the digital screen.

"And the girl?" The voice over the intercom, the sound delayed, reminded me of the old Japanese Kung Fu movies. It was asked with a note of disdain. Here among this group of men, where the bloodlines are matriarchal, there was blatant offense.

I looked over at Jace's sister. She seemed as oblivious of the proceedings as I, though she sat straighter as the group as one, turned and acknowledged her presence. Even the old guy on the main screen turned to look at her, but it was cursory at most, as if she were a means to an end.

"What of the other matter?"

The sound delay brought a smirk to my face. Everything was a bit surreal and I couldn't help but imagine myself in one of those movies and any minute a horde of black-clad ninjas was going to burst into the room and a violent melee would ensue. My eyes wandered over to the large double doors through which I had come. Two formidable looking sentries stood stone-like on either side, hands crossed in front of them, giving further credence to the possibility of a horde of ninjas.

My captor leaned forward a bit, his voice hesitant. "Unfortunately, the situation concerning the old blood has deteriorated." He straightened in his seat. "They have taken two, killing them outright, and Garrow narrowly escaped with his life."

"Garrow?' I said it before I even thought. I looked at my captor and then scanned the attentive faces surrounding the table. "Mr. Garrow's alive?" The sudden realization that he was one of them rocked me. *Son of a bitch.* I sat back hard. Could he have saved my mother? Did he know about the dangers? Was he the danger? Every eye was on me with my outburst. I tried looking defiant but inside I didn't feel it. I felt small, helpless. They may defer to the man on the screen, but they exuded power in their own right.

I wished Jace were here. He'd know what to do. I glanced over at Jace's sister. The resemblance, especially in the eyes and her lips, was obvious, so much so, I was surprised I didn't connect it at our first meeting. Admittedly, I was a bit distracted. I scratched the back of my head and looked down as she caught me staring. Her lips brought to mind the kiss and then one thing led to another and I was reduced to fidgeting in my seat, too many images flashing through my mind, images of her and Jace intermingled.

Where's a ninja horde when you need one?

"But, we can proceed?" It sounded like a question, though the authority of the question left but one answer.

Several of the council members looked directly at me, while others shared conspiratorial glances with the old man beside me.

I glimpsed movement out of the corner of my eye and the double doors opened silently.

Garrow's eyes scanned the room then landed on me. There was no hint of surprise. He knew I was going to be here.

"Ah. Mr. Garrow. I do hope you've recovered."

Mr. Garrow nodded, looking directly at the digital screen. He rubbed absently at fresh scars; white puckered flesh on the back of his left hand that traveled up under the cuff of his sleeve. I noted another scar on the side of his throat and dark purpling where someone had grabbed him and possibly tried to choke the life out of him. For all his wear and tear, however, Mr. Garrow seemed none the worse; quite to the contrary, his countenance practically glowed with vitality. He stood tall and there was an indescribable boldness, an air of insolence about him. He didn't acknowledge the individuals in the room and ignored my captor who stood as Garrow approached the table.

"How will we proceed?" Garrow spoke directly at the screen. "The Blackwell retaliation will be swift." Garrow glanced at me. "He is of great importance to the family."

I felt their singular attention, a tangible weight of curiosity. What bothered me was the notion that I was the reason they were all here. I wondered who they were and studied them as covertly as I could. None looked familiar; nothing about them exceptionally significant. They all appeared to ignore their fellow cohorts. Their body language spoke volumes, a lack of familiarity and unaccustomed to being in such proximity to each other. It brought to mind a meeting of adversaries, a meeting that would surely not end well.

CHAPTER TWENTY-SEVEN

The Blood's Corruption III

Jace

"What's going on?" Since my earlier outburst things had grown just a little bit sketchy around the Blackwell homestead. I couldn't help but think of an anthill or a beehive; so many people coming and going. I didn't recognize most of the faces, but a few stood out; one of the police officer's, the "bad cop" that interviewed us after Trystan's mother's death, the reporter: Jason Steele, who wrote about the series of murders and the security guard at the high school were among the numerous guests currently holed up in my father's study.

My mother had been on the phone practically non-stop and every minute or so I could hear another car drive up to the house.

My mother waved my question away, gesturing for me to leave her alone. My glare went unnoticed. A pair of clergy, one definitely catholic, the other of the new non-denominational variety strode purposefully towards my father's office. I suspected there had to be at least 20 people in there by now. I glanced furtively at my mother who spoke quietly, but urgently into the phone.

Her suggestion that Trystan was alright, because they knew where he was, seemed to be losing validity. It occurred to me then that these people were the makings of a rescue party. But that would mean that they were all vampires too or at the very least familiar with our situation. Though I was leaning heavily towards vampires.

I inched my way toward the closed office door. From where I stood, I heard nothing. Unusual for a riled bunch of bees or ants, I surmised. The closer I got the more perplexing was the lack of noise. Finally I pressed an ear to the door. Still nothing. I quickly hid. Another duo, this time two crossing guards, one who worked in front of the high school, walked directly to my father's office. The office was big, but certainly not big enough to hold close to two dozen people.

The door, mounted on casters, slid quietly in and out of the wall, instead of swinging open and closed. It was thick and heavy, but even as the door was open, neither sound, nor voice carried from the inner office. I tried to peer into the room, as the door slid closed, but wasn't quick enough to see anything but the corner of his desk and the big easy chair in the far corner.

I approached the door again, leaned in, and then glanced in both directions to see if anyone was coming. I don't know why I was skulking around my own house, but I did get the feeling that I was not invited to this little soiree. I couldn't help but be a little put out by the notion. Trystan was my boyfriend after all. Certainly I had every right to be in there to discuss how to get him back. I nodded my head, reaffirming my own conclusion then reached for the door. To say I tried and failed valiantly at making a grand entrance would not be an understatement. The door slid as quietly as intended, no loud dramatic bang, except for the one I made as I slammed into the door. It slid rather slowly and I was impatient.

The office was empty.. "What the....?"

I glanced around as if those two dozen were playing a little hide and seek, much like Trystan and I used to play when we were little. My father's office was one of out favorite places to hide. It was so quiet. I turned slowly until I'd done a complete 360. No one was in here. I examined the walls, pushed and pulled on light fixtures, even leaned the big easy chair on two legs to look under it for a secret passage: nothing. I sat in the chair to think, staring blankly out into the hall.

It occurred to me then that my father never let us close the door to his office. While he never denied us entrance into the office he warned that the lock was broken and if we closed it we might never get out.   My father is a gentle man, but when the need arises, he can be foreboding, even menacing. I shook my head. Surely, it wouldn't be as simple as that. I stood and walked to the door and pushed to close it. It didn't move, much like the few times before when I didn't heed his warning about the lock. I examined the door. A small groove had been worked across the width of the door. I ran a finger along the length of it until it met the wall. There was a small pressure button fashioned seamlessly into the wall. I pressed it and the door slid on its own volition. I felt an out draft of cool dry air and looked to my left.   As the door slid closed on one side, it slid open on the other revealing a brightly lit set of stairs leading down.

A voice drifted up, angry and menacing like nothing I'd ever heard, rallying and threatening simultaneously. It was my father's voice. I took a step back. *Maybe I shouldn't go down there. Maybe...* I took another tentative step back when the door to my father's office started to open again.   My search for a hiding place was a frantic one, nothing like my searches as a kid with Trys quick on my tail.

"Mr. Blackwell."

I stopped dead in my tracks. I recognized that voice. The scenario notwithstanding, my pounding heartbeat quickly led to the recognition. I turned slowly. Mr. Callahan, our illustrious high school principal stood stoically in the doorway. My shoulders sank. This was not good, no matter what I might say in rebuttal, coming face to face with the principal always brought out what could easily be deemed my worst qulaities..

I opened my mouth in greeting but what came out was incomprehensible. I looked left then right, for a route of escape, but there was only one open to me. I dashed down the stairs and knew without looking back that Mr. Callahan followed at a much slower pace.

At the foot of the stairs a dimly lit hall split left and right. I did a quick double take over my shoulder then sprinted to the left. The voice that I heard earlier rang clearly in the corridor and when I rounded the corner I stopped at the spectacle before me.

For the most part vampires appear normal; otherwise we'd never be able to blend in so seamlessly. The truth of the matter, our condition was not the frightful visage seen in the movies. Quite to the contrary we appear rather mundane, albeit a bit healthier, a little more perfect. The campaign to vilify us has been in the making for centuries. If you must know, it's our scent, technically the pheromones. The *scent* is different in so far as it is more potent, more animalistic and the biochemical reaction is immediate and acts much like a hallucinogen. It induces fear.

While vampires have an innate immunity, the overwhelming cloud of it amidst so many left me trembling. I began to turn, to flee; the fight or flight instinct kicking in, but then I felt a hand clamp down on my shoulder. I might have yelled out but from the back of the chamber a piercing wail of anguish rose up. Rising up on my toes, I tried to look past everyone in the room.

I stepped back unconsciously, my breath caught in my throat. For once, I was elated Trys was not with me. At the far end of the room, shackled by a long heavy chain was Trys' mother, not quite dead any more.

CHAPTER TWENTY-EIGHT

A Rising Tide

Jace

"What the Hell?" I looked at Trys' mother; she pulled at the binding chain, her wrists bloody and raw, then at my father. Her wail had quieted but there was urgency in her task to be free. She noted my presence with a renewed effort, the chain rattle, a surreal backdrop to the otherwise silent room.

My father glared with consternation then gestured, quickly flicking a finger, and before I knew it, I was hustled out of the room and up the stairs and planted rather firmly in the easy chair in my father's office. I marveled at the notion that my father; mild mannered and unassuming, held that much power, that with a mere gesture; men jumped. There was so much I didn't know.

My mother stood in the office doorway as the entrance to the hidden staircase closed.

"Did you know?" I rose abruptly.

"Jason." My mother seldom referred to me by my birth name but when she did, it was never good.

I sat back down feeling the weight of her gaze. "Did you?"

She nodded and stepped into the office. "We didn't know it would happen. The Old Blood is intent on chaos, determined to bring about our downfall, in any manner possible. Striking at us this way." She paused and looked out the bay window that lit the room. "They have great enmity for the Blackwell name. Their last confrontation resulted in my parents death."

I looked up, astonished. I knew they had died in a fire, but was told it was an accident.   My mother remained stoic in the revelation

"I believe their intention was to turn Trys which is why he is safer with the Blood Council. His protection is paramount, though it may not seem so to you."

"He can't know that she's been..."

My mother nodded. She took the remaining steps between us cautiously. "Jason."

The weight of her gaze was crushing now. "You know what they intend."

I nodded. "I don't want..."

My mother laid an arm on my shoulder and sat on the arm of the chair. "It could mean the end of the hatred. The end of so much needless death."

"There's not another way?"

She smiled tenderly as she shook her head.

"In the end, the choice will be his to make."

You can lead a horse to water....

I remembered how he was when he mentioned her kissing him. Even more I remember the sudden jealousy I felt when he told me. Because I could see in his eyes a want, a lust; something he shouldn't have been feeling with my mark.

"I'm afraid." I don't know if that was an accurate description of what I felt. I knew he loved me. We've been inseparable as long as I can remember, but the idea of losing him to her ignited a fear, a trepidation that I couldn't describe in any other way.

"Don't be. You've an innate connection with Trys that I've never seen before. It goes beyond love. If there was ever a definition for soul mates, I see it in the two of you."

"A connection is not the same as... What if she's meant to be with him? I mean what we have is the most natural thing in the world to me. I have...loved him for so long. But what if it's wrong. What if...?"

"What is meant to be is meant to be. And I know, in my heart and soul, that the two of you are meant to be together. I can give you no hope that you don't already carry in your heart.

What you feel is true. You have to believe in it. Your doubt, your actions, will prove to be your undoing. Fear is destructive if it is given strength. Fear builds walls."

I felt the fear now. I shook with it internally. Listening to her strengthened my resolve, but her words gave my fear strength of its own; making it more real.

My mother stood and held her arms open. "Come here." I stepped into her embrace and a calm washed over me. "Do not be afraid." She whispered. "You are my light and my strength and I will not see you hurt, no matter the cost."

I sighed in response, shuddering as the fear diminished to a distant memory.

We both turned at the sudden out draft. The door slid aside and a cadre of vampires stood waiting for the door to finish opening, my father at the fore.   My father stepped forward and my mother wrapped arms around him and pulled me into the embrace.

My father stepped back then and held me at arms length. "You mustn't tell Trystan of his mother. At least not yet."

I nodded in agreement and looked at my mother who smiled at his reiteration of my own words. "I know."

The last of the stragglers exited the stairwell and the door closed. The exodus of vampires was quick and silent. I'd forgotten anyone else was there with us, despite the obvious crowd around us. My father started after them but he paused at my words

"What about the others. Will they... " I looked at the closed door.

"We are assuming the worst. The Old Blood intends to destroy us. We must believe there will be more than the few we are aware of. There will be a great rising, if history is any indication." He drew my mother close to him and I wondered if they thought of my grandparents killed in the fire. "If I thought I could send you away without you returning, I would. As it is, I can only ask that you stay here." He eyed me and I stilled my rebuttal.

"Where are you going?"

"We go to the Blood Council. They have important information. I'll retrieve Trystan and bring him home to safety, if I can." He looked at my mother. "And our daughter."

My mother stiffened in reaction. "We can only hope what damage has been done can be undone."

The pain in my mother's eyes was overwhelming, though she stood straighter and nodded. He kissed her quickly and pulled me into a quick hug before following the last of them out of the office. My mother watched after him, long after he was gone she stared blankly.

"What do we do?" I waited in the heavy silence. "Mother?"

Her eyes rounded, realization moving her to action. She inhaled deeply. "We prepare for the worst. Come."

I couldn't help but imagine my mother from another age, another place; an Amazonian, tall and fierce, a warrior queen as fierce as any man. What was at risk was her family, her very existence and in her stance, her mien, was a determination that brooked no dissent.

I followed quietly as she strode up the spiral staircase to the third floor. At the far end of the hall was a seldom-used guest bedroom. Spartan would best describe it, a bed, and a single lamp upon a utilitarian bedside table. A long mirror covered one wall. I watched mystified as my mother ran her fingers along its edge where it met the wall. Here too a button was worked seamlessly into the wall. A subtle click and she slid the mirror aside, revealing a cache of weapons. Guns; pistols, rifles and shotguns, and a variety of blades, short and long, lined the wall. I fear had I seen a row of stakes I might very well have laughed aloud, but nary a splinter of ash or yew was in sight. I stepped back as my mother selected a shotgun and in one quick smooth motion chambered a round. I didn't have time to marvel at the act as she held it out to me. It was heavier than I expected, the double barrel cold, shiny and pristine. She selected several handguns and I half expected her to sight down the barrels, like on TV, aiming at nothing and everything, but instead she grabbed a box of ammunition, paused, then grabbed another. She turned me deftly towards the door, staying me for a moment with a firm hand on my shoulder before handing me what had to be the largest knife I'd ever seen, sheathed in an intricate worked-leather case. She nudged me from the room, pulling the door closed behind her.

I wondered what other mysteries this house held as I walked hurriedly down the hall. I'd lived here all my life and Trys and I had played in every room, as kids, yet I'd had two surprises in one day. Was I so smitten with Trys even then? The idea made me smile because the very notion was a surprise, itself, a wonderful one.

We walked the length of the hall and came out in the library.   I looked over the railing, noting the secret collection of books. They covered the desk; a large pile of them had slid to the floor. My mother walked past with nary a sidelong glance and strode to the French doors overlooking the grand balcony and yard below. Her attention was complete as she scanned slowly from left to right. I edged up behind her and she glanced back for just a moment and produced a smile, but it was cold and forced and didn't reach her eyes.

CHAPTER TWENTY-NINE

A Rising Tide II

Trystan

Truth, like beauty, is in the eye of the beholder. What one views as truth someone else will view as a corruption of the truth. Politics and religion are two fine examples of such a dichotomy. Who's right and who's wrong is determined by perspective and knowledge. Knowledge itself has its own dichotomy and interpretation delineating right and wrong.

I drew a finger across the scar, tracing the edges of it. I'd had for so many years; it was a part of me and the truth of it was up for debate. Did it save me, or in marking me, had Jace condemned me to my circumstances? He'd expressed as much himself. Had he not marked me, chances are I would be dead; I would have died right then and there, under the bows of that tree. But having saved me, he diverted the path of my life and everything that happened afterwards was a result of my salvation. But some would say, had I never met Jace, I never would have been in that tree and never would have fallen and he would not have had need to save me. What is the intersection of our lives that determines the direction of our path? Was all of this predestined; merely a preset path yet traveled?

The doors were remarkably quiet and she stood watching me. I only noticed her, catching slight motion out of my peripheral vision. I looked up, startled. She wore a dress of flowing green gossamer fabric, draping sleeves to her wrists.

Her smile, a smile I was very familiar with was almost identical to Jace's. I tried a smile myself, but it felt halfhearted at best. I couldn't help but wonder what she thought of everything. She drifted slowly into the room, her steps hesitant, stopping more than once before determination forced her to my side. She stared down at me for a moment, unspoken questions in her gaze.

"What are they like?"

I knew of whom she spoke, it would have been a question on my mind as well, but I waited for more.

"The Blackwells."

Not *my family my parents, my brother.*

She didn't sound like Jace or her mother, which is something I had thought she would. There was an otherworldly sound to her voice, something foreign, her articulation, short and abrupt. She waited for a response.

'They're family." My answer came unbidden.

She winced, the words striking her.

I wanted to take it back. I realized it was an awful thing to say, but the words were truer now than ever before. I had grown up in their house, had been a second son to them and yet my words were cruel.

"I hate them."

Slumping back in my chair; I hadn't realized I had sat up as she approached, I nodded. What could I possibly say? Surely, I could not negate her feelings. What she must believe, what truths she had been told. I yearned to tell her everything, to share my memories, but I held my tongue. My memories should have been hers and each of them would be another verbal strike felt deep inside.

"They didn't know." I spoke earnestly. "They thought..."

She shook her head. "Don't." Her eyes were closed as she shook her head, but the word was commanding.

I wanted to convince her; illuminate her to the truth but our attention was drawn to the door. We both watched expectantly, but no one entered. She returned her gaze to me.

"Can I tell you something?"

I nodded. The earnestness in her voice was hypnotic. "Sure."

When I bit you..." she paused for a moment and looked at the door again. Then back at me. "They sent me after you. They told me I could change you. Told me you were important. I didn't believe them but I wanted to try." As she spoke her voice hardened. "To please him." She looked to the door again. "I knew... I knew he wasn't my father. But he raised me as such. Or so I thought." I could tell as she spoke, she believed what she said, validated by her truth, her experiences, the life she had lived. I wondered what it had been like. Was she a groomed pawn, manipulated with lies. Truly they had to be lies, even if they were unspoken. The old man had raised her for what? Knowing who she was, what path was he leading her down. "After I bit you, I felt..." She looked away, fingers to her lips as if reliving that moment. "...Something. But nothing happened. *He* had marked you. Protecting you from the change. My father...he was surprised. Though he didn't show it, the truth was in his eyes. I've learned to read it, to feel it." She shook her head, her eyes focused on me again. "You were a surprise to him, a boon to his quest."

She didn't speak for a moment and a sudden sadness filled her gaze. The silence was heavy.

"I became an afterthought, pushed aside." The vehemence and conviction in her voice pushed me down. I tried to sit up straighter as she loomed over me. She glanced furtively at the door again then slowly pulled a blade from beneath the draping fabric of her sleeve.

"I thought it would be enough."

My confusion must have shown on my face. She smiled, not like earlier; hesitant and demure. This hate-filled smile blossomed quickly. She put her fingers to her parted lips and I could see the fangs. It was almost theatrical, the way they slowly became evident. Her pallor suddenly flushed crimson, her eyes lit brightly, pupils dilated and her nostrils flared. I was mesmerized by the transformation. The girl before me was an intoxicating beautiful creature filled with a malevolence that was undeniable.

"She thought she recognized me when I knocked on the door. I looked familiar. And I have to say; she tasted nothing like you as I drained the life from her. But I savored it"

She held the blade to my throat and I could feel a line of blood tickling its way down my throat.

"Before you die, I want you to know. Your mother is my child. She died once, but before I kill her again, she will know that I killed her child too." She pressed the blade harder and I held my breath, my eyes watering at the exquisite sting of the knife's edge. "You will have nothing more of mine and *no one* will have you."

CHAPTER THIRTY

A Rising Tide III

Jace

The old man threw a quick glance in my direction. Something in his expression rattled me.

"What are you doing here?" I stared balefully, "Where's Trystan?" My voice was raw. I had to find him. I didn't know why but I felt an overwhelming urgency that battered my thoughts.

"You need to come with me now. It may already be too late."

My mother stepped in front of me. She pointed the shotgun at him her other hand guiding me further back.

"Too late for what."

"We've no time for niceties. If you don't come with me now, Trystan will die."

"What did you do?" I backed away from my mother's guiding hand and rushed around her, stopping in front of him. I had unsheathed the knife and now held it to his throat but he didn't even flinch, only held his arms wide and bared his neck.

"Do it, and he will surely die. Our goals are one and the same. You may not believe me but his survival is paramount. And this show of bravado will do nothing but bring about his death. " I could see my own eyes reflecting back at me on the blade.

"Jason. Step away from him." My mother's voice was calm but firm.

I shook my head, even as I stepped back.

"We don't have much time." My actions didn't seem to faze him in the least. Quite to the contrary his presence proved to be a distraction.

I heard the catch in my mother's breath and turned to see her disarmed and two large men holding her. She didn't struggle and her eyes remained on me. She nodded.

We'd heard their arrival, or rather heard the old man, we were just unaware he hadn't come alone.

He'd arrived in an extravagantly long limousine that sat idling in the driveway as we approached. A large man stepped out and opened the door for the old man and I.

I sat quietly, watching the house as it disappeared in the evening gloom.

"Don't worry about your mother. She'll be perfectly fine. I imagine she could easily disarm and overpower my assistants if she thought you were in any real danger."

I looked at him.

His grin, though not malevolent, still held an air of darkness that didn't alleviate my worry.

"Do you know who you are, Jace Blackwell?"

I nodded absently.

"Truly?" His smile widened and he stared with expectation.

"What do you mean?"

He waited for more, silently glancing out at the passing countryside. When he looked back at me I saw something in his eyes that startled me, something I recognized, though in all honesty, I didn't know what it was, just something innately familiar.

"You are the progeny of a long line of vampires, a dynasty, some might say, that goes back almost a thousand years. A millennium of history flows through your veins, a history that has been coming to fulmination. Some view you as a catalyst, but in all honesty, the catalyst is your Trystan."

At the mention of Trys, I was suddenly alert. He saw my curiosity captivated.

"You and he..." He shook his head. "Fairy tales." He laughed.

I'm sure I appeared perplexed by that.

"The Old Blood view you as a messiah. Christ come again, so to speak, to bring them out of the darkness, literally. There's this notion of the dark ages, *saeculum obscurum*, in history and literature. It's used in a pejorative sense, though in all actuality it refers simply to a lack of intellectual writings of the time and not to any literal darkness or malevolence. But there is a truth to it of course in that pejorative notion. That lack of writing, viewed by the historians of the time was due to a purging."

His voice had taken on a note of recollection that seemed to diminish his presence in front of me; as if part of him travelled back. I could see the glow of Fairweather off in the distance reflecting off a ceiling of low clouds and reflecting in the tinted glass was his reflection, an apparition.

I didn't know why he was telling me all this. What it was, this history so to speak seemed irrelevant to my current situation and I felt a bit of aggravation.

His laughter drew me back. "I can see you must have been an unparalleled student in class."

I frowned at that.

"Oh don't take offense. You've the appearance of many a student I'm quite certain. I'm certainly not expecting your rapt attention despite everything." The old man paused a moment, a look of consternation crossed his face and as if in response the driver sped up. I don't know if it was coincidence when I felt a sudden stinging at the base of my neck. The old man watched me, appraising me, it seemed.

He gave an almost imperceptible nod.

The car turned quickly onto a dark graveled surface and, while the sound was muted it startled me. I looked out the tinted window and up on a hill, as if taken from every cliché movie one could imagine was a large structure, a mansion. The gravel quickly gave way to smooth paving drawn down the length of a manicured lawn. Large hedges lined the perimeter of the estate easily ten feet high. The house itself towered above the hedges and a couple of the windows glowed amber, two eyes peering out into the darkness over the hedgerow. As we approached the manse, the doors slowly opened, a beastly maw, with brightly lit sconces shining like bone white fangs.

My neck burned, the stinging burn of a razorblade drawn quickly across skin. My breathing grew labored and I could taste blood, the tang of it flooding my mouth. I felt my fangs expand against my gums and a surge of adrenaline rocked my every sense.

Instead of reaching for his door, he reached across me as the car came to an abrupt stop in front of the house and opened my door. "It's time you saved him again. *Now.*"

The cold air hit me quickly and it was as if I'd come out of a fog, one that had deadened my senses. But with the emphasis of that one word, *now,* my senses came alive like never before. I could feel everything; the old man's heartbeat, ancient and strong, the airy scent of night blooming flowers and somewhere close by, blood. It was an eternal instant that found me in a doorway, my breath caught in my throat as I took in the scene before me. Trys, had a deathly pallor and a fearful expression etched upon his face; his eyes distant and staring blankly. Somehow, even in this state, he noticed my presence and turned towards me, one hand bloodied as he attempted to staunch the wound at his throat, reached for me.

In that moment, another eternal moment that I'd never forget, I howled in anguish. I was at his side in an instant and took him in my arms, the pain that I often felt when touching him flared unbearably. I staggered but held onto him.

"Trys. Trys. Trys." It was my mantra. "No. No. No." The anguished words I heard but didn't realize I was saying. I was disconnected from my being and fully invested in his life and it was as if I saw the whole thing from above, outside of myself. I shook my head and though I closed my eyes against this visual assault I could still see it against my eyelids. I could hear his heart, the weakest of pulses and I flashed back to that instant in the forest so many years ago.

I felt his hand, cold fingers gripping feebly at my arm and he looked at me, his eyes flat and almost lifeless. His lips moved but no words came forth. His grip grew stronger and he shook my arm for attention and I watched his lips move again. *I love you.*

Time stopped. I leaned in and kissed him. His lips moved against mine as if he continued speaking those three words. I couldn't see, my tears blurring everything.

When I bit him, I staggered, as if the very earth shook violently beneath us. I felt his grip tighten around my arm and a fire flared deep within me that burned so painfully I cried out and fell to the floor. I took great gulps of air, not to breathe but to extinguish that pain that burned so excruciatingly within me.

"You see child."

I looked over my shoulder. The old man stood, a blurry apparition. "It was so written." The old man stared off as if reading the words in the air. "And a dark child shall be borne in a deep well of fire and blood."

The end of
Book One

Coming Soon
❖
Book Two: Once Bitten
Book Three: Last Bite

Also available from Nicholas Scott

❖

A Kiss Is Just a Kiss

Chapter One: First Kiss

"So yeah. I just want to try it." Aiden Pike was an Adonis.
Simply put, one of the most beautiful guys I'd ever seen.   And he
knew it, not that *I* thought he was beautiful, but that pretty much
everyone thought he was beautiful.   How we had become
friends in the last couple of weeks is a mystery to me.   I'll admit
I had a sneaking suspicion that there was some sort of bet going
on behind my back, à la Cruel Intentions.
"Let me get this straight.   You, Mr. Popularity, Mr. I-Can-Have-
Anyone-I-Wanted, you, want to kiss me, Cody Beaumont?"
His smirk was to die for; that mouth, those lips, beautiful and
mesmerizing.
"Well, I normally just go by Aiden, but yeah, I want to kiss you."
He grinned devilishly, leaning against the wall, his nicely
sculpted abs peeking out from between the bottom of his t-shirt
and the top of his jeans.
"Why me?" Don't get me wrong, sure I was cute, but in
comparison, well, there was no comparison.
"Why not?" He countered casually. He stared directly at me, his
eyes boring into mine.
"Sweet talker." I meant it to come out stronger, but the words
tumbled out, a choked whisper, losing the irony I intended.
Aiden rolled his eyes. "Hey, it's a win-win situation."
"Win-win?"

"Yeah" Aiden put a hand on his chest. " Look, I know." He took a step closer. I tried to look away but he had me mesmerized. "I've seen the way you look at me." He leaned forward and whispered, his breath tickling my neck, his lips grazing against my ear "You practically rape with me your eyes."
I blushed. It was true. I couldn't count the number of times I'd undressed that boy in my mind. It didn't help that he had no modesty, none whatsoever. The first time we hung out, this was like right before classes started up again and we were over at my apartment. He was slumming it. The complex has pool and he wanted to use it. Why, I don't know, because his was Olympic size. I had to force him to put on a pair of my swim shorts. Course that didn't stop him from dropping trow, right in front of me, not a care in the world. And by the end of the afternoon, he was swimming buck-naked while I was walking around with a giant towel wrapped around my waist, hiding my excitement.
"How about this. You let me kiss you and I'll let you suck me off. Y'all like that sort of thing."
I didn't know whether I was suddenly excited or pissed off.
"Y'all?" I looked at him, incredulous. *He did not just say that!*
"Yeah fa." He stopped himself as I quirked an eyebrow. "Come on, you know what I mean." He tried to laugh it off.
 "First off, you arrogant prick, the fact that you're asking *me* to kiss *you* is pretty fucking gay. Second, believe me when I tell you, if I were to suck you off, not only would you like it, but you'd be begging me to do it again and again."
"Hey I'm just asking you for a favor and giving you something in return." My boastful bragging seemed to have no effect on him. He took two steps back and had the audacity to pull his t-shirt off. His abs were perfectly sculpted, the definition so exquisitely chiseled, I couldn't help but stare. His arms, shoulders, chest; they were all flawless. I was actually drooling. I swallowed, searching my suddenly bloodless brain for a retort, a quip, any sort of witty reply that might negate my jaw dropped reaction to him.
"You want me Beaumont. And you can have me, just this once, for a kiss." He undid his jeans and let them puddle around his ankles. He was going commando.
"Come on!" I croaked. This was not happening.

He reached across the two steps between us and took my hands pulling me closer. He placed one palm flat against his chest. I could feel his heart beating, slow, steady and strong. He took a deep breath then guided my other hand to his cock. I felt it growing, hardening in my grasp. "One kiss." He teased. It was just a whisper. Reaching behind me, he untucked my shirttail and rolled the shirt up, as well as the ribbed tank top underneath.

This was not happening. I kept saying it over and over in my head, but was unable to speak the words aloud.

He was fully erect in my hand as he wrapped his own around mine, his big palm warm. Slowly he began thrusting in our grasp. A glistening bead of precum seeped from the tip of his cock. He moaned as he rubbed the ball of his thumb across the sensitive head.

With a skilled hand he finessed my jeans open and let them drop. He slipped a hand inside the waistband of my Calvin Kleins and I shuddered as he deftly sent tremors quaking through me.

In my wildest of dreams, I couldn't imagine anything more erotic, more sensuous. I leaned into him, relishing his excitement, desperate to give in to his request. His lips glistened and I wanted nothing more than to taste them. He slid his hand around the base of my neck and drew me into the kiss.

I couldn't help but wonder if he'd done this before. It was a foregone conclusion that he'd been with girls. There were stories and at least one illuminating iPhone video to validate his heterosexuality, but the ease at which he yielded to the kiss, the eagerness at which he accepted my tongue; there was a familiarity to his actions that seemed too natural. I couldn't help but wonder about the sex. Being impaled, feeling his weight on top of me, his teeth biting me, his fingers digging into my hips. I moaned into his mouth as he kissed me hungrily. The kiss was over before I knew it. I stood motionless, my face upturned, breathless. Aiden's eyes were closed and to me, he never looked more vulnerable. I leaned in to kiss him again.

Bright Lights, Black Rainbows
A Fairweather High Novel

Chapter 1: Ethan

I'm a fake. A fraud. A poser. A nobody. And I like it that way. Nobody knows me... well almost nobody. Most everyone thinks they do. One look at me and images and ideas plop into their minds like crap and they think they know me. My black hair and pale skin, my thin lithe body and I hear the whispers; *Goth, freak, emo* ... but they don't know me. They hate me, want to hurt me, want to make me disappear because of who they think I am. The truth in their minds is the biggest lie. They don't try. They don't want to try. It's easier if they live in their own little worlds and hate or fear what they don't know. They're robots and fakes and posers too. But they don't think so. Fashion plates of popularity, facades to hide behind, afraid of who they are, but comfortable in their own skins because they are accepted by their peers. To hell with their peers, who don't know who themselves either. It's a vicious cycle. Spiraling down and down till it's too dark to see anything other than what's behind their eyes and not in front of them. Living their Stepford lives. The mainstream is a sluggish bloated river filled with the detritus of the popular. What pains me most is I want to dive into it, and drink it and live it and be accepted by it. As I said, I'm a fake, a poser and I want nothing more than to be accepted by at least one of them, to be known, inside and out, to be grasped and embraced by someone who might just see beyond everything else, beyond the lies and facade and see in me, who I really am. Because I don't know.

I heard the knock on my door and I knew it was probably my sister. She's never one to get the hint when I had the door closed and the music turned up.

"Ethan?" It was my mother. I rolled over and clicked the remote and turned off the music. My mother took that as her signal. She opened the door with some hesitancy and poked her head in. "Is everything all right?

I couldn't help but roll my eyes. Why do they always ask that when it was obvious, blatantly obvious, that no, everything wasn't all right. The world was shit, everything was crap but they seemed to think everything was just fine. Or at least wanted to hear it.

"Yeah I'm great. School just su..." My mother's eyes rounded a bit. She wasn't used to the new phase that I was going through. You know, teenage rebellion and all that crap. Just another label to explain away whatever angst or anger or misanthropic notions I might be going through "...Wasn't the best first day, is all." She seemed suddenly relieved. This was familiar territory for her. She could have her patented heart to heart about how school, like everything else, was a necessary part of life and you had to make an effort to fit in, to be accepted. I imagined little birds singing and her wearing an apron like the mother from Leave It to Beaver or some other 50s show.

I'm an enigma to my mother. She doesn't understand my isolation. It's beyond her comprehension. Her stories of high school, the cheerleader, the valedictorian, club president this, prom queen that; I was an ironic little twist thrown into her life. I could tell she struggled with it and it pained her to see me alone. But she, like everyone else, had her facades, her role to play. So she propped me up, tried to relieve my pain in the only ways she knew how.

"Well if you need to talk about anything, I'm right here." She tried to smile reassuringly, but I think she felt she didn't know what she'd be getting into if we had a true heart to heart.

"Okay." I looked towards the window again and clicked the remote and The Great Escape by Boys Like Girls poured from the speakers. I heard her pull the door closed. I closed my eyes and listened and thought it fitting. We didn't understand each other. Opposite sides of the same die, no matter how it's rolled, we're both looking the opposite way. Young or old, guy or girl, popular or not; we could never see eye to eye, no matter how we tried.

If your own mother didn't know you, who would? I realized this was not fair. My mother knew me in the ways that mothers do. She knew when my room was a pigsty, she knew when I'd sneak a smoke out on the roof. She knew when I drank milk from the milk carton; the things that mothers know, these things she knew but like I said, we didn't get each other. Her perspective on my life was through the rose colored glasses of pompoms and football games and late nights down at the local hang out, wherever that was.

I picked up my cell phone and started to text Billy. *I need you.* I cancelled the text and dropped the phone and looked back towards the window. In a perfect world, he'd be knocking on my window right now, his smile bright, his eyes mischievous, an unlit cigarette hanging from his lips waiting for me to climb out onto the roof and light one up with him. I drew a finger across my lips, imagining his lips on mine, his weight pressing down on top of me; comfortably, and his excitement, obvious with his grinding, his breath on my neck as he lay his head on my shoulder, his eyelashes brushing my cheek.

I rolled over and buried my face in between my pillows, imagining him nestled next to me, whispering in my ear that he loved me, that he missed me. That he wanted me back. I could only sigh, knowing it was just wishful thinking. We were over. His parents had seen to that and then his friends.

All summer I had struggled to get over him. And it was working, in the way that time alone works. No simple reminders, no pictures, no him, till he slowly slipped from my mind.

But we had plans for the first day back to school. Big scandalous plans of walking hand in hand down the hallway, maybe a lust-filled kiss before parting to our separate classes. And that stand and be proud confrontation before whatever asshole thought, maybe, they could call us fags, and get away with it.

Billy was a dreamer; strong in words, but weak in spirit. High in hopes but low in strength. When we talked about it, nestled together under the comforter, our arms wrapped about each other, our breathing slowly calming down, our heartbeats evening out, our sweat chilling except under those down blankets, it was always about how we were different. We would show everyone. There was nothing wrong with our love. There was nothing wrong with us. His eyes glistened with hope. He wanted to believe himself, as I did.

I think we are never more afraid, than when we are in high school. We are learning about who we are. Being pulled this way and that. Acceptance and peer pressure, the cliques, the popularity, the friends; everything an ingredient buffeting against who we think we are already. It's confusing, it's frightening, not on that conscious level, but deeper. And we don't explore ourselves that deeply. We're not afraid or confused. We're pissed. We're angry. We want to kick someone's ass.

"I don't understand." I looked at him. *His eyes, those deep brown, almost black eyes looked at me, imploring me to understand.*

"Ethe. She said I couldn't see you. She doesn't think it's a good idea. Too many people, the football team... If they found out..."

"So everything you said, about how we would show them? That was bullshit?" I pulled my arm back as he tried to reach for me. It took everything in me not to go to him, to be in his embrace. I wanted to cry. But I was pissed. "You're just a fucking coward. All talk!" I pushed him. And for a second I was a little surprised thinking what the fuck am I doing. I love him. But then I pushed him again. "Get the fuck out!" I pushed him again and he hit the wall next to my bedroom door. A picture of the two of us our arms draped over each other's shoulders with cigarettes hanging loosely from our lips, crashed to the floor. We both looked at it for a moment.

"Ethe. I love you."

"You love me? If you loved me, you wouldn't, at the first sign of trouble, want to break up." I reached up and angrily wiped tears from the corner of my eye. Fuck him, he wasn't going to see my weakness. "If you loved me, you wouldn't want to break up cuz your mommy said it's not a good idea."

"Ethe?"

"Fuck you, Billy. If anyone found out? What happened to our big plans? People weren't going to find out. We were going to show them! Remember?"

"Ethe, my dad..."

And that was almost enough. I almost stopped there. His father was brutish and a drunk, filled with his own insecurities. Forcing Billy to take football and soccer and baseball hoping it would make a man out of him. "I'm not gonna have one of them sissy boys under my roof." he would say after one too many beers. And hopefully that would be the last of it, but other times he would hit. Blacken an eye, bruise a rib. I'd seen it twice, one time waking, to find him outside my window, his cheek swollen and red, his eyes pleading for sanctuary.

We'd slept together that night for the first time. His touch tentative, at first, caressing my face, kissing my eye lids. His weight, light atop me as we kissed, afraid that he might crush me. As if he weighed a ton or something. I pulled him down, and he collapsed atop me with a nervous laugh. I kissed him harder and that was all it took. He pulled at my shirt and didn't even mess with the belt and zipper as he pulled at my jeans. We ground against each other, kissing frantically. and I whispered to him. "Fuck me."

"I ... I haven't."

"Fuck me Billy." I pulled at him, grinding my hardness against him. His eyes were a bit ravenous. But he'd never had sex before. I grabbed his cock and he groaned.

"I want you to fuck me with this." I whispered in his ear and gave his cock another squeeze. I maneuvered under him and positioned him. "Go slow."

"I... I haven't."

I pushed my ass back and the head of his cock pushed at me. I groaned. Mentally reminding myself to get some lube. His hips seemed to go into automatic pilot as he pushed back at me and I felt him enter me.

"Ahhhhh! Fuck. Slow! Slow!" Against my own words, I pushed back against him and felt him go in deeper. It burned and bit my pillow. And pushed back again.

Billy grabbed my hips, and thrust. "Oh shit.'

My muscle tense, my back straining against him as he tried to pull out. I reached back and pulled him to me, until he was completely inside of me. "Now stay." I panted. "Let me get used to it."

Billy leaned forward and kissed my back, my shoulder blades. I turned and looked back at him and he kissed me. "Does it hurt?"

"Fuck. Yes. But. Don't. Stop." I had to breathe deep with each word as he started to drive into me; his grip on my hips, tight. He pulled me back to meet each thrust. He leaned down and wrapped his arms around me and thrust deeper. His breath on my neck gave me chill. "I love you Ethan." He grabbed my cock and jerked in time with each thrust. I panted heavily and pushed back to meet him. "I want to see your face." I almost screamed when he pulled out of me.

He thrust back into me and saw the pain on my face as I lay on my back, my legs propped against his chest. I almost laughed at the sight of my feet splayed as they were, my toes curled in ecstasy. His thrusting grew more heated, one hand grabbing at my chest, the other gripping me tight, jerking faster with each thrust. I was delirious; my head thrown back, my breath shallow as I came closer and closer to a climax.

"Oh God!" We both screamed it at the same time and I felt his cock expand and shoot inside of me. I had a moment to think CONDOMS! before I shot all over my chest and cheek. He leaned down and kissed me, licking at my cheek and kissing me again. We tasted sweet. I felt his heart beating as he lay atop me. No care to crushing me this time, his exhaustion winning out. I welcomed his weight, his presence. I tightened my embrace around him, the slick mess between us forgotten. I kissed him again and again and again, thinking I could never stop. It was like breathing, something I had to do.

#

"You need to go, Billy." My heart was pounding in my chest. Remembering that first night together; I was weak for him. I wanted to be mad. I wanted to scream at him. But I also wanted him to fuck me. Right then. Right there. I turned away from him, walking towards the window. I pulled my cigarettes from my

pocket and knocked one out of the pack, then climbed out my window.

"Ethe?"

I didn't look up as I closed the window. I saw him out of the corner of my eye, his shoulders hunched. I knew he was crying, I could hear him through the glass. I perched myself below my window, watching the smoke curl around the moon. I didn't look up when I heard his car start, I didn't see the yard flash in his headlights, I didn't watch as his break lights disappeared out of sight at the far end of the street. At least I tried not to, but I saw his silhouette under each haloed streetlight. This time I didn't wipe the tears from my eyes.

There was another knock at my door, but no hesitancy this time. My sister opened the door and ran and pounced on my bed. She was 8 years old and had more energy than a thousand Chihuahuas on crack. She snuggled up against me. "School sucks!"

I couldn't help but laugh. "Get used to it."

"Cindy Masterson called me ugly."

That killed my laughter. I looked at her and smiled. "You're my little monster and nobody can call you ugly. Besides you're beautiful." And she was. She looked like my mother, a cheerleader in the making, with her big blue eyes and wavy blonde hair. Almost predetermined. "Hey, you want that I should break her knee caps for ya." My Italian accent was horrible enough to make her laugh and she laid against my shoulder as I turned off the stereo and turned on the TV. She grabbed the remote and turned it to the Cartoon Network. I sank against my pillows and sighed.